The Witch of Godstow Abbey

Murders in the Abbey Series

Book Two

Lady Harriet &

Dr. Peter Stephenson

THE WITCH OF GODSTOW ABBEY

This was a work of fiction inspired by historical events and family stories. Names, characters, places, and incidents were products of the author's imagination or were used fictitiously, with some names changed to protect privacy. While certain historical elements were based on true events, the narrative had been fictionalized to explore themes creatively and was not a literal account of history.

HARDCOVER ISBN: 978-1-964700-49-6
PAPERBACK ISBN: 978-1-964700-50-2
EBOOK ISBN: 978-1-964700-51-9

First Edition
Historium Press, a subsidiary publishing house of
The Historical Fiction Company
New York, NY / Macon, GA USA
www.historiumpress.com

Table of Contents

Dedication

Most of us first learned history back in our school days. The emphasis was on names and dates. Boring for many. However, history is a never-ending story, full of intrigue, fascinating people, and events. That is the way Jack Rackam teaches it. He does it in peppy, occasionally irreverent illustrated bites of just a few minutes on YouTube and Patreon.

(https://www.youtube.com/@JackRackam)
(https://www.patreon.com/c/jackrackam/posts)

We dedicate this book to our favorite historian and teacher…

Jack, this one's for you.

Dramatis Personae

Lady Harriet FitzAlan – 21st Century

Lady Harriet of the 21st century is a descendant of the 14th century Harriet. She is a researcher in genealogy and medieval history and lives in Clevedon, England. She is based upon the co-author of this book, the real Lady Harriet, a Lady of the Manor under English law, and a descendant of Charlemagne.

Sister Agnes

Sister Agnes is a Benedictine nun living at Godstow Abbey. She is the abbey's infirmarist, supervising the activities of the abbey's infirmary. She is an accomplished healer, herbalist, nurse, and anatomist. She becomes involved in solving the crime of murder using 13th-century forensic medicine.

Isabel de Beauchamp

Isabel is a young lay sister at Godstow Abbey, home of Benedictine nuns. She works in the infirmary under Sister Agnes. She aspires to take her final vows and become Sister Catherine.

Mother Alice de Gorges

Mother Alice is the Abbess and Mother Superior of Godstow Abbey. She was a real person who served from 1295 until her death in 1304. There appear to be no portraits of her. This portrait was generated using artificial intelligence text-to-art. Our character, Mother Alice, struggles to develop a good working relationship with the abbey's infirmarist, Sister Agnes.

Lady Beatrix de Aylesbridge

Lady Beatrix and her noble family are benefactors of Godstow Abbey. She has developed a close friendship with Sister Agnes and will assist her in solving crimes. Beatrix, an only child, was orphaned as a young girl when both of her parents died suddenly from dysentery contracted at a gathering of noble families, leaving her the mistress of the de Aylesbridge estate and fortune. However, there were whispers that her parents' deaths were not accidental, leaving Beatrix committed to solving crimes of murder, hoping to uncover the real cause of her parents' demise.

Undersheriff Alric the Bald

Alric, a fictional character, serves as the undersheriff of Oxfordshire, overseeing most local investigations and law enforcement duties. He reports directly to Sheriff Henry de Thisteldon—a historical figure who actually existed—who manages the county's administrative affairs.

Alexis, Bard of the Shire

Alexis is an Irish Celtic bard and seer. She wanders Oxfordshire with her family, including her maternal grandmother, who also is a seer. She prophesies through her songs and stories. In Book 1, *The Whispering Dead of Rewley Abbey,* a trespasser on the king's land appears to have killed her. Now she miraculously returns to aid Agnes, Beatrix, and Isabel in the search for the witch. A real person who is, at the time of this writing, a young singer/songwriter, inspired the character of Alexis.

Friar Thomas de Glanville

Friar Thomas de Glanville is a *Dominican inquisitor in disciplina.* (an inquisitor charged with matters of Church discipline). He comes directly from Pope Boniface VIII, with orders to investigate possible heresy in Oxford, generally, and particularly at Godstow Abbey. As an *inquisitor in disciplina,* he is responsible for enforcing correct practice and belief, as well as ecclesiastical and doctrinal discipline.

Mamo, Alexis's Grandmother

Mamo, meaning "Mother" or "Mom," is Alexis's closest relative. She travels with the family, and Alexis claims that she inherited "the sight" from her. She is an herbalist, healer, and midwife. She and Sister Agnes laboured to save Alexis, shot with an arbalest bolt in Book 1 – *The Whispering Dead of Rewley Abbey.* Like most Celts, she worships the "old gods and goddesses".

Professor Reginald Barrington

Professor Barrington is a lifelong academic, educated at Balliol College, and a noted world traveler and scholar. His areas of expertise include civil and ecclesiastical law, with a particular focus on heresy, church doctrine, and the interpretation of heretical symbols and texts. Sister Agnes and Lady Beatrix seek him out as an advisor in these matters.

Martin, the Stable Hand

Martin is a middle-aged man who works for the abbey as a stable hand. He is generally unkempt with poor personal hygiene. He is known for his persistent pursuit of women and chases after any woman he can find, except the abbey's sisters. He is not particularly intelligent, and he has some very disagreeable connections.

Mary Wood

Mary Wood is a fictional character. However, she is based upon a very real person, Mrs. Mary Isabelle Wood, who was both the cheerful and capable librarian and the inspiring 7th-grade English History teacher at a private girls' school in Indianapolis, Indiana.

Edwin de Ravenswold

A knight and lord, Edwin de Ravenswold descended from an old family. The oldest of local legends spoke of a battle—a day when a king's knight, grievously wounded, had fallen. As the enemy pressed forward, a great black raven descended from the sky, alighting upon the knight's shoulder. The knight rose, wounds forgotten, and the tide of battle turned. Victory won, and in gratitude, the king granted the knight vast swaths of land. He descends from ancient Celts and eventually joined *The Kindred*. Finding their blood rights anachronistic, he formed *The Circle*, a gentler sect based upon old Celtic ways.

Lady Harriet FitzAlan – 13th/14th Century

In the 35th year of King Henry, she assumed the title of "Lady," granted by the king as partial payment for the heroic deeds of her brother, who had been lost in battle during the Crusades. She also inherited his estates and fortune. Having no siblings, she was one of a few medieval women who operated a manor and its possessions in her own right rather than assisting a man, such as a brother or father.

Introduction

Lady Harriet FitzAlan sat in her study carrel at the Bodleian Library in Oxford. A mature, widowed academic, she had long nurtured a passion for medieval England and the genealogical treasures hidden in the university's vast archives. The Bodleian, with its collection of over 8,000 medieval manuscripts and centuries-old atmosphere of hushed scholarship, beckoned to her often from her home in Clevedon.

She enjoyed the stillness of libraries, especially this one, with its soft scent of parchment and leather. Left with independent means by her late husband, Harriet could afford to linger as long as she pleased, lodging nearby at the charming Old Parsonage Hotel. Each morning, she pulled her cloak of Scottish wool tightly about her and made the short, familiar walk past St. Giles Church and the Eagle and Child pub, into the heart of Oxford.

Now, having shed her cloak and straightened her long braid of silver-gray hair, she leaned over a vellum folio dated to the closing years of the 13th century. As she turned the pages, handling each carefully and with reverence, a strange story began to emerge. Not one recorded in any modern account, but one whispered between the lines: a tale of nuns and novices, of heresy and dread, and of a sect known only by a dark name—*The Kindred*.

Harriet leaned closer. This was not merely history. It was a mystery.

And so, our story begins.

BOOK THE FIRST
THE SINS OF A NOVICE

In which we learn of mysterious illnesses
and other strange goings-on in the abbey,
and a novice commits heretical acts
outside the chapel door.

Chapter 1
Bones of the Innocent

In which we learn of the startling discovery of what appear to be infants' bodies that shakes the Godstow community. Isabel reflects on the past. Mother Superior, alarmed, tasks Agnes with uncovering the truth about the dark events affecting the abbey.

It had been an especially warm autumn following close on the heels of a hot spring and summer in 1299 Oxford town. But now, the air had shifted. A crispness lingered in the mornings and at eventide, a quiet herald of the cold to come. Kneeling in the dirt of the infirmary's herb garden, Sister Agnes and Lay Sister Isabel were hurrying to get the wintering-over herbs in the ground, assuring a fresh supply when Spring arrived. Agnes, as the infirmarist of Godstow Abbey, saw to the growing and harvesting of the herbs to be used as healing potions.

Garlic, sage, chamomile, calendula, and foxglove were all important for Agnes's collection of herbs for her infirmary. As she prepared the soft earth to receive her plantings, she meditated on some of her herbs. Foxglove was very important. Used to treat her older nuns who had illnesses of the heart, this potion needed to be used with care. Calendula, Agnes used on rashes of the skin. As she dug, she prayed to various saints who would help her seeds grow into healthy herb plants she harvested for her workroom.

Saint Fiacre was the patron saint of gardeners and herbalists. Hildegard of Bingen was a Benedictine abbess known for her expertise as an herbalist. And, of course, she could not complete her

11

garden without a prayer to St. Benedict, the patron Saint of her order of Benedictine nuns.

The autumn sun was starting to set, signaling that it was time to leave the garden, perform their ablutions and go to the chapel for Vespers. But before they could move, Isabel's voice rang out from the far side of the garden, screaming again and again, "Sister, Sister, come quickly!"

"What on earth is it, child? Are you injured?"

Isabel was breathless. "No, Sister, no. But you must come. Hurry!" And the screaming broke out once more, raw with terror.

Agnes walked rapidly around to the other side, where Isabel was on her hands and knees, a garden claw waving wildly in her hand. There on the ground in front of Isabel, half buried in the soft, freshly-turned earth, were three tiny bodies.

Pale and shaking, Isabel could scarcely speak. She tried to catch her breath, but to no avail. "These are b… b… babies, sister. Wh.. wh… who would kill newborn infants like this?

"Sister, compose yourself," said Agnes firmly, as she knelt to examine the tiny grave. "These are not human babes. They are piglets. Still, I would know why they were buried so—and by whom. Go you now, and fetch me a blanket to wrap them in. We must not cause alarm within the abbey."

She stood and looked Isabel squarely in the eye. "Then go to Mother and ask her to meet me in my workroom. But collect yourself first. If any see you thus, there will be questions — and we must not give rise to idle fear. Go quickly, but with care."

Sister Agnes – The Piglets

Sister Agnes took the three small bodies from the towel in which Isabel had wrapped them and placed them gently on her worktable. "Isabel, return to the garden and fill in the grave so that it won't rouse suspicion among our sisters. I'll see to Mother when she arrives."

"Yes, Sister. Immediately."

Taking the towel, Agnes rinsed the dirt from it with clear water and then, with the damp cloth, she cleaned the dirt from the piglets. No sooner had she completed the task than the abbess entered her workroom.

"Good evening, Sister. What can be so urgent that you have summoned me just before prayers?"

"Look you, Mother. We found these three small piglets buried in my herb garden. And, if you look closely, you will find their throats slashed. There was no blood in the grave. Mother, someone sacrificed these piglets and drained the blood from their tiny bodies!"

"What can you mean, 'sacrificed'? In some sort of ritual?" The abbess was incredulous.

"Forsooth, Mother. But how they came to be in our garden, I cannot fathom."

"Did you find them, Sister?"

"Isabel found them and, thinking that they were babes, took fright and summoned me. I went to her and examined the grave. I saw at once that they were not babes but piglets. I sent her for a towel in which to wrap them and then to request that you come to the infirmary and see for yourself."

"I am deeply troubled, Sister. There can be but one explanation, and that is that there are demon worshipers about. But amongst our sisters. I can scarce credit it — yet we must be certain, I warrant. See you to another search and do so with discretion. We must not raise alarm. Mayhap there is some simple cause behind this outrage."

"Mayhap, Mother. I will see to it… discreetly." However, doubt stirred within her.

"Now to evening prayers, Sister. Hide the bodies where they'll not be seen, until we may lay them to rest in a more fitting place."

Isabel – Reflections

As Isabel covered the grave of the three tiny piglets, she reflected upon the past and her hopes for the future.

Autumn of 1299 marked nearly four years since Novice Isabel had, albeit unknowingly, aided in the murder of a university lecturer and her own father — at the hands of her brother. For that grave sin, she had been sentenced to a year of penance.

Thanks, she believed, to the support of Sister Agnes, her mentor in the abbey infirmary, Isabel had eventually been permitted to return. Not as a novice, but as a lay sister.

Isabel accepted the decision of the abbess and had worked hard over the past five years to learn her art in the infirmary and to make herself right with her God and her sisters. Along the way, Lady Beatrix, a highborn noblewoman and a close associate of Sister Agnes, had seen fit to include her in various investigations—or 'searches for truth' as Mother Alice called them—in which she and Agnes collaborated. Now, Isabel was a full part of the 'team' with Agnes and Beatrix. While the abbess was nervous about their inquiries, she tolerated them as long as the investigations were discreet. Discretion was one other thing Isabel had learned and learned well.

During those five years, Beatrix had revealed to Isabel a truth: that Isabel herself was of noble birth. But Isabel chose to set it aside. She had given herself wholly to God, to Godstow Abbey, and to the quiet life of their small community. She had no need for the privileges or trappings of her lineage. Now, at the age of twenty, Isabel looked forward to the next steps in her journey to sisterhood at the abbey. She had experienced much in those five years. Several inquiries had been a focus of her training, emphasizing her native talent for logical thinking, reasoning, and deep observation.

Though Isabel was preparing for the day when Agnes, now thirty-two, might retire to a life of peace and contemplation, she could not imagine the abbey without her. Agnes had been her guide and teacher from the beginning. Whether showing her new ways to diagnose ailments among the sisters or drawing her into strange investigations with Beatrix, Agnes had always been at her side. But, for now, she was Lay Sister Isabel, hoping for the coveted name of Sister Catherine, her choice should Mother Superior allow her to take her vows as a nun. Taken from the martyred saint, Catherine of Alexandria, the name represented the blend of intellectual and spiritual dedication to which Isabel aspired.

But she knew the discovery of the three piglets would weigh heavily on her mind. It had clearly unsettled Sister Agnes — and Mother Alice as well. What none of them could have foreseen was how deep the inquiry would go, or the terror and depravity it would uncover.

Sister Agnes – Rumours

Sister Agnes was in her workroom when Mother Superior entered quietly, as if she wanted her presence there kept secret. "Sister Agnes, how did our sisters learn of the piglets? The rumours are everywhere, and I cannot fathom how." Mother was not happy.

"I have no idea, Mother. Isabel and I have been very careful – very *discreet* – about the incident."

"It is obvious that there has been a slip somewhere. Somebody besides you and Isabel must know of this. Are you certain that the two of you were alone in the garden when you made the discovery?"

"Reasonably certain. I will address this matter, Mother. When I discover the source of these rumours, we will be able to quench this fire of doubt that some of our sisters seem to be fueling."

"See that you do, Sister." The edge in Mother's voice was, if anything, sharper than when she entered the workroom. "Quickly, and…"

"Discreetly. Yes, Mother. Of course."

As Mother Alice left the workroom, eyes blazing, Agnes stood for a time contemplating the problem. For problem it certainly was. She never had seen the abbess so disturbed. As she meditated upon the rumours, Isabel entered.

"Sister… what troubles you? I can see that something is not right. May I help you?" Isabel was surprised, if not shocked, by Agnes's demeanor.

"Isabel, what know you of rumours within our walls about the piglets?"

"Well, I have heard some sorely vexing talk, whispered in shadow," Isabel said. "But nothing certain."

She looked uneasy, clearly concerned, yet had no answers to Agnes's query.

Just then, a novice entered the workroom, her face tense. "Sisters. My Lady Beatrix begs leave to speak with you. It is urgent."

This bewildered Agnes. She had not expected a visit from Beatrix this day. "Do show her to the garden. Isabel and I will join her anon."

"Very well, Sister," and the novice departed hurriedly, her gray wool habit rustling as she ran, to escort her charge to the abbey's gardens.

It was a pleasant late afternoon in the Oxford autumn of 1299. The warm sun hung low in the sky, casting long shadows, while a gentle breeze stirred the trees in the abbey gardens. Beatrix had already arrived, accompanied by a novice. Sister Agnes greeted her warmly as the novice stepped back, out of hearing's reach.

"Well met, my lady, and what brings you to our abbey?"

Beatrix's agitation was plain. "You've not heard, Sister? There's talk in town, gossip, no doubt, that the sisters found the bodies of three babes, their throats slit, buried in your herb garden. Can it be so?"

Sister Agnes – Calming Explanations and Serious Concerns

"My lady, there is no need to fret so. Come, sit you here and let me tell you all as it is." Agnes then called for the novice, bidding her fetch a warm draught to the garden. "Come, let us sit by this stone table and await our refreshment. There are no babes, Lady Beatrix, but I have much to tell you, and we have God's work to do. Serious work."

Lady Beatrix, an ardent supporter of the abbey and friend to Sister Agnes these many years, spent much of her time assisting with investigations into disruptions of the peace in the ecclesiastic community, in particular, and Oxford town in general. Working together with Undersheriff Alric the Bald and Isabel, the four had solved the grisly murders perpetrated four years past by a mad killer, believing that he, cursed by the ghost of his first victim, was under the supernatural protection of "Lord Saturn".

The murders ended with the killer's violent death. His body was burned, the ashes cast to the four winds. After a time, the town settled back to its normal routine, and the loathsome murder spree carried out by a madman drifted into the stuff of children's tales.

The key that unlocked the clue leading to the truth behind the murders came from a young Irish maid, Alexis — Bard of the Shire — who, folk said, had 'the sight.' Whether it was true second sight or simply a sharp intuition, the four never knew. A poacher on the king's land shot her with a crossbow after she stole his poached game from the cookfire.[1]

The novice arrived with the warm drink, and Agnes, well acquainted with both Isabel and Lady Beatrix after so many years, poured each as she knew they preferred: a splash of milk and honey for Isabel, plain for Beatrix. Agnes herself took a touch of honey in her small earthenware cup before beginning to recount the tale of the piglets and Mother Alice's unease.

"My Lady, what I needs would share may have weighty consequences for the abbey and our faith. The bodies uncovered by Isabel were not babes, but newborn piglets. What is more, someone slit their tiny throats as if in a sacrifice. Mother Alice is gravely

---

1 See *Murders in the Abbey – Book 1*: <u>The Whispering Dead of Rewley Abbey</u> for the whole story.

concerned that these piglets died in a ritual touched by evil, though its nature is uncertain. That alone is troubling enough, but the quest before us also asks how came they to be buried in our herb garden?"

Beatrix was pale, her hands shaking slightly. "You cannot mean this, Sister. How can it be? Are there demon worshipers abroad within the abbey?"

"I know not. But Mother has demanded that we uncover the truth and cleanse this scourge from our presence by what means we must. I will enlist our confessor and the professor from Balliol to assist us, but we must do this swiftly, in quiet, and with discretion. We must ensure that Mother knows every step we take. Isabel, you will keep a faithful record of our inquiries both for Mother and for the undersheriff should we uncover that which he must report."

Agnes paused, deep in thought. "There is much that we must do to prepare. This is a perilous task upon which we embark. We must seek the guidance of the confessor at once. Isabel, go you to the chapel and see if the confessor is there. If he is, bring him back at once. Mother's concern weighs heavily upon us."

Chapter 2
A Garden's Secret

In which we learn more of Sister Agnes and the discovery of poison plants in her herb garden, raising questions of intentional cultivation. Agnes performs an autopsy on the piglets and learns the disturbing facts of their deaths. Rumours and whispers within the abbey begin, leading Mother Superior to increase her pressure on Sister Agnes and Lady Beatrix.

Sister Agnes reflected on the theft of pages from her copy of the *Picatrix* four years earlier. As she recalled, the pages had contained information on several herbs and the potions that one could mix using them. One or two stood out in her memory. Chickpeas and olive pits were, of course, harmless. But others stood out as deadly poisons. Among these, aconite—known also as monkshood—was particularly dangerous.

There were those who confused aconite with other poisons, such as 'alcondiz,' a term Agnes had encountered in her studies referring to a deadly substance from Armenia. However, Agnes, educated by skilled herbalists, understood the difference.

Sister Agnes – An Autopsy

"Isabel… fetch you the bodies of the three piglets. We must discover how they died. Mayhap by sacrifice. Mayhap not. We shall see."

"Yes, Sister. The bodies are beginning to corrupt, even with the cool autumn weather. We must make haste."

Isabel carefully placed the three small bodies on Agnes's worktable, laid side by side with gentle reverence. What stories that simple wooden table could tell—a chronicle of ailments cured, lives saved and lost, and secrets revealed from the dead. She then fetched her writing desk, prepared to set down all that Agnes bade her record.

Agnes bent over the bodies, her magnifying stone in hand, inspecting each piglet with meticulous care.

"Isabel… these piglets did not die by the blade. Look at their snouts. See the foam about their mouths and the blue tint of their lips? These piglets were, I suspect, poisoned before they succumbed to the blade."

"But with what, and by whom, were they poisoned, Sister?"

"As I recall from the stolen pages and from our copy of Dioscorides' *De Materia Medica*, there are several poisonous plants that could account for these signs. The blue tint to their lips matches the hue of the flowers on monkshood, and the foam about the mouth aligns with what is known of its effects."

"But why would someone do this to such tiny, helpless creatures?" Isabel's voice quavered, her eyes glistening.

"Look you closely at the cuts to their throats, Isabel. Do you see? There is little humour flowing. Now, take my magnifying stone and examine the edge of the wound. Do you see that small puncture near the neck? I believe these piglets were victims of a sacrifice. First, the executioner gave them a potion, perhaps made from monkshood, to dull their senses. Before life fully left them, the executioner drew their vital essence through that puncture, likely made near one of the great vessels. Only after he drained their essence and the poison overtook them, did the executioner slit their throats."

Isabel gasped softly. She was near tears. "But why, Sister? Why would someone do such a thing?"

"As to 'why,' I know not yet. If it was a sacrifice, there must have been a ritual. The draining of the humour points to a blood offering. Such a gift would serve to appease or honor a god—or perhaps a demon."

Agnes straightened, her face lined with concern. Her frown deepened, and the wrinkles around her eyes bespoke the weight of her analysis. "I must away to Mother. She must know of this at once." And before Isabel could answer, Sister Agnes was gone.

Sister Agnes – Mother Alice

The abbess sat in her chambers, reviewing the abbey's ledgers. Sister Agnes entered without waiting for the novice outside to announce her.

"My child! What urgency drives you to burst in so?"

"I must tell you what I've found, Mother. It is deeply troubling."

"Then speak, Sister."

"The piglets did not die by the blade alone. They were prepared first with a potion—I suspect monkshood, judging by the blue tint of their lips and tongues. Before death took them, the executioner drew their vital essence through a small puncture wound near one of the great vessels. Finally, he cut their throats — not as a killing blow, but to bleed them wholly, leaving not a drop of life-humour behind."

"A sacrifice to the Devil, then?"

"Yes, Mother. I believe that this is the work of those who serve the Enemy."

"You must see this matter to its end, Sister. Nothing is of greater importance. Should these demon worshipers take root here, they could bring ruin upon us all. Forsooth, the sisters already speak of evil in the abbey. That must not be allowed."

"At once, Mother." And Sister Agnes left to return to her workroom.

Isabel awaited her return. "We must bury these piglets, sister. Where should we take them?"

"There is a hedgerow down by the river. We shall lay them to rest there close to the Creator who made them and beyond the reach of those who profaned their little bodies."

Sister Agnes – A Walk in the Garden

Sister Agnes was troubled—deeply so. The chill of the autumn air only seemed to deepen her unease, yet she resolved to take a quiet turn about the abbey garden and mull over her churning thoughts. She sought no particular purpose, only the solace of walking amidst the fading flowers, the hedgerows, and the hardy winter herbs that clung to life in the cooling earth.

Drawing her habit closer against the sharp breeze, she walked toward the herb garden. Here it was that Isabel had stumbled upon the sacrificed piglets, a discovery that still weighed heavily upon Agnes. She slowed her pace, her eyes drifting over the familiar winter plants.

She sought nothing in particular, yet something unfamiliar caught her gaze. A tall, hooded plant with dark leaves and pale, purple-blue flowers stood starkly among the orderly rows—*monkshood*. Agnes's breath caught.

How had such a thing come to be here? Monkshood, a plant of deadly poison, had no place in her garden. Neither she nor Isabel would have dared to cultivate it.

Her thoughts churned as she stared at the toxic intruder. Who had brought it — and why? Steeling herself, she turned and made swiftly for her workroom.

As usual, Isabel awaited her. "Sister, you seem greatly troubled. What weighs upon you? What has vexed you so?"

"You must come with me. I have something of great import and mystery to show you."

Isabel pulled her heavy wool cloak over her novice's habit and made ready. Together, nun and novice walked as briskly as the chill winds would allow to the herb garden.

"Now, Isabel, look closely at the garden. Do any of the plants seem unnatural or out of place?"

"Sister… what is that purple flower? I've never seen its like before."

"That is monkshood, Isabel. It is one of the deadliest plants known. How came it to be here, in our herb garden?"

"I know not, Sister. I have never seen it here before."

"And when last were you in the garden?"

"Only yesterday, Sister Agnes."

"And it was not here then?"

"No, Sister Agnes. It was not. Forsooth, I would have marked it, for its petals are most peculiar."

"Then I would know who was here and planted this. Fetch my gloves and the spade. We must uproot this poisonous invader with care. Do not touch it, and mind you keep its parts away from our herbs. Once we remove it, we shall burn it well away from the abbey and our garden."

Chapter 3
Illness in the Abbey

In which mysterious ailments afflict several nuns in the abbey, leading to growing suspicion of a sinister force at work, as one of the sisters dies.

In her workroom, Agnes continued to think about the piglets. Buried safely now, certainly something was amiss, with poisonous herbs, animal blood sacrifice, and, still a mystery, the theft of pages from her Picatrix these five years past. Her thoughts wandered to the rumours among her sisters and the townsfolk. The nuns in the abbey community, ill at ease and troubled in spirit, put their faith in God and the Blessed Virgin. Still, Agnes had no answers and had yet to form a plan to get them.

Sister Agnes – A Turn about the Garden

As Agnes sat at her worktable, the door to the workroom quietly opened and Isabel entered. "You look troubled, Sister. What ails you this forenoon?"

"I am troubled, Isabel. I know not how the monkshood came to be in our garden, and I fear that there may be more baneful herbs lurking there as well."

"Mayhap we should look, then, sister. A turn about the garden may help to put your mind at ease."

"Aye, 'tis so, Isabel. Forsooth, it may."

"Do you know what it is we seek, Sister?"

"Nay, Isabel. I know not."

Pulling their cloaks tightly about them against the autumn chill, Agnes and Isabel stepped from the warmth of the workroom into the crisp air of the abbey gardens.

"There be many gardens here, Sister," Isabel murmured as they passed beyond the herb beds. The convent's vegetable garden, where the nuns grew much of the abbey's food, lay beyond, now mostly bare. Across the grounds, the flower garden, though not large, offered blooms for feast days and sacred observances.

They walked in measured silence, the cold biting at their skin as they scanned the frost-bitten plants. Most of the vegetables had begun their retreat into the earth, their leaves brittle and brown in the grip of approaching winter. Yet amid the withering stalks, something caught Isabel's eye.

"Sister, look you there," she said, her voice sharp with discovery.

Agnes turned to where Isabel pointed.

"See yon leeks, Isabel? And beside them—parsley, or so it seems. Yet I mislike the look of it. The leaves are close the same, yes, but look at the edges: too finely cut, and the green too pale. This be no kitchen herb, Isabel. This be Fool's Parsley—bane to any who eat it." Before Isabel could respond, a novice came running toward them, breathless and stricken with fear.

"Sisters, come at once! Sister Sophia is most grievously ill! She cannot move, and I fear..." The girl gasped for breath. "I fear she is dying!"

Sister Agnes – Sister Sophia

It was but moments before the three women arrived at Sister Sophia's bedside. Upon the small wooden table lay a half-eaten bowl of soup, the surface long cooled, as though abandoned. At once, Sister Agnes spied the telltale green of what appeared to be leek leaves and parsley floating in the broth.

"Isabel, take you the scent of this soup."

Isabel bent low, breathed in, and hesitated before shaking her head. "I smell nothing. I smell nothing, Sister."

Agnes's expression darkened. "Forsooth, Isabel. These be no simple herbs. They be the selfsame plants we spied in the garden but moments ago—Fool's Parsley, and Fool's Parsley be a killer."

Isabel gasped. "But… 'tis but parsley! It looks the very same."

"Aye," Agnes nodded grimly. "Yet true parsley bears a fresh scent, clean and sharp. Fool's Parsley holds no such fragrance and therein lies its treachery. Those who mistake it for a harmless herb find it to be their doom."

Turning to the young novice, Agnes gave her command.

"Go at once to the kitchens and fetch a jug of warm saltwater. Bring also mustard seed."

The novice curtsied swiftly and was gone before Agnes had scarce finished speaking.

Agnes then turned to Isabel. "Isabel, whilst the girl fetches the saltwater and mustard, go you and make ready a draught of wine steeped with rue and garlic. Mix it well, then add angelica root. It shall soothe her belly and quiet the spasms."

Without another word, Isabel, too, was away, disappearing into the dim corridors that led to the depths of the abbey, where the stillroom and kitchens lay.

Agnes took a clean cloth, dipped it in cool water from the pitcher, and placed it gently against Sister Sophia's forehead. The elder nun stirred at the touch, her breath still coming in ragged gasps.

"Hush now," Agnes murmured, pressing the cloth lightly, hoping to ease the woman's shaking. "The draught shall soon bring relief."

Moments later, the young novice returned with the warm saltwater and mustard seeds.

Agnes turned to the novice, "Hie you to my workroom and bring my mortar and pestle. We must grind these herbs fine before we can make the draught."

Placing another cool cloth upon Sophia's brow, Agnes murmured a prayer for healing, entreating the aid of Saint Benedict and Saint Raphael the Archangel. As she whispered the final words, the mortar and pestle arrived, and without delay, she began to prepare the mustard seed infusion to help purge the venom from the stricken nun.

Isabel returned with the warming cordial, but ere Agnes could administer it, she bid Isabel hasten to the herb garden and fetch fennel and mint.

The warm draught of water and mustard seed drew forth the poison. Once Isabel returned, Agnes took the fennel and mint leaves, placed them in the mortar, and ground them fine. As with the warm water, she pressed the infusion to Sophia's lips, gently urging her to drink.

Soon, the sickness abated, and the spasms eased. When Agnes saw that Sophia no longer trembled, she gave her the cordial that Isabel had prepared. As warmth returned to her body, her breath steadied, her hands unclenched, and at last, she slept.

Sister Agnes – Back to the Gardens

Sister Sophia's affliction troubled Agnes. True, the nun was among the eldest in their community, yet she had ever been hale, her humours well-tempered and in balance. That she should fall so grievously ill was unsettling.

The presence of Fool's Parsley in the garden, and now in Sophia's soup, gnawed at her thoughts. Had the poisonous herb found its way there by mere mischance, mayhap through the carelessness of a kitchen nun? Or did it point to something more sinister? Worse still — how had it come to be in the garden at all?

There was but one course of action.

"Isabel, fetch you your cloak. We go at once to the gardens. I must know if yet more of these baneful plants have found their way into our cloistered grounds."

"Aye, Sister. I be ready."

Isabel wrapped her rough-spun gray cloak close about her, the hood pulled low over her head against the chill winds that raked the abbey walls.

She picked up a basket to collect any plants that should not be in the garden.

Out in the gardens, the winds had gathered in force, and the smaller trees bent their boughs beneath the bitter icy blasts.

Kneeling on the cold earth before the vegetable garden, both Agnes and Isabel searched carefully among the withering stalks for any unwelcome intruders.

"Forsooth, Isabel, there be plants here that I know not." Agnes pointed to several that lurked among the vegetables and cooking herbs, their presence almost unseen. She frowned, her mind reaching back to the stolen pages of the *Picatrix*, taken from her library four years past, and the deadly herbs it recorded.

"Look you, Isabel. See this one, with its shriveled black berries and the last remnants of a purple bloom? Though the frost has withered its leaves, there be no mistaking its nature. This is Deadly Nightshade, a poison most potent. A mere taste of its fruit can bring death."

She gestured toward another plant, this one standing apart, its once golden flowers now withered by the chill. "And this—Henbane. It, too, is a perilous thing, known to steal the senses and still the breath. We needs must remove them from our cloistered grounds. But heed me well, touch them not with your bare hands, lest the poison seep through the skin."

Taking care, the two women uprooted the plants, wrapping their hands in cloth before placing the deadly greenery into a basket, to burn ere nightfall.

Sister Agnes – More Illness

Back at the abbey, Agnes and Isabel slipped out of their heavy cloaks, setting the basket of poison greens upon Agnes's worktable.

"Touch them not, Isabel. These be of mortal danger, even through the skin. I must examine them and learn their origin."

Carefully setting the basket aside and covering it with a clean cloth to keep its deadly contents from prying eyes, Agnes gathered her tools—her magnifying stone, her vials of purifying tinctures, and her shears—for closer study of the plants. Yet, as she made ready to go to the chapel for prayers, a nun entered in haste, her face pale as linen.

"Sister Clare! What troubles you so? You look as though you have seen a specter."

"It is Sister Margaret, Sister! She is raving about the devil in her chamber and cannot rise from her chair. You must away to her at once—'tis as if madness has taken hold of her!"

The two sisters moved swiftly, Isabel just behind them, to the side of yet another stricken nun. As they entered Sister Margaret's chamber, the young woman, barely past her simple vows, sat rigid in her chair, her breath labored. Though it would be several more years before she took her final profession, she was yet young and impressionable at twenty years of age.

With a look of concern, Agnes stepped forward and raised her hands in a gesture of reassurance.

"Hie away, Sisters! Enter not! The de'il is with me, and he'll drag ye doon tae Hell!" Margaret's thick Scots burr tangled her words, her voice high with fear.

"Peace, Sister," Agnes soothed, her tone low and steady. "There is none here but us. See you?" Slowly, she inched closer to the trembling girl.

Margaret's chamber was a simple, spartan space. A rough-hewn bed stood against one wall, its mattress stuffed with straw. A plain cabinet held her habits and other modest garments. Beside it sat a straight-backed wooden chair, where she now rested, and a small table stood nearby. Upon the table, a cup of ale, a half-eaten piece of rough bread dipped in honey, and a small wedge of cheese lay untouched.

At once, Agnes's gaze sharpened. Now she knew what ailed the young sister. It could be naught but henbane, one of the deadly plants she and Isabel had gathered from the garden. The poison had likely been mixed into the dough, passing for rough-ground flour before the loaf was set to bake.

With careful hands, and without drawing notice, Agnes wrapped the half-eaten loaf in a clean linen cloth, setting it aside to bear to her workroom for closer examination.

"Isabel, hie you to the kitchens. There, prepare a draught of saltwater and crushed mustard seed. Grind the seeds well ere you mix them, and bring the jug to me anon." Without another word, Isabel hastened to do as Agnes bade.

Turning then to Sister Clare, Agnes spoke with grave urgency. "Sister, we shall have need of a draught made of charcoal and wine. The charcoal will draw forth the poison and restore balance to her humours. Then, steep you another cup of wine with rue, garlic, and angelica root. All are well-marked in my workroom."

"At once, Sister Agnes." And without delay, Sister Clare set forth to fulfill her task.

Whispering a prayer of healing, Agnes approached the stricken young nun. With soothing words, she bade Margaret join her in entreating the Blessed Virgin for peace and healing. The girl's lips moved, though barely able to form the words. Her thick Scots burr blurred her speech, yet Agnes took heart—for Margaret was calmer now, the stiffness that had seized her limbs beginning to ease.

Isabel soon returned with the mustard seed infusion. Though Margaret struggled to swallow, she managed most of the draught. A tremor ran through her body, and at length, the potion did its work. Agnes and Isabel then guided her to her bed and urged her to rest.

Presently, Sister Clare returned bearing the two potions she had mixed at Agnes's instruction. Together, the three women helped Margaret drink. As warmth returned to her body and her breath grew steadier, the fear faded from her eyes. The storm within her quieted, and at last, sleep took her.

"When she wakes, Isabel, give her a little broth and some milk with honey to restore her strength," Agnes instructed.

With that, she made haste to the kitchens, determined to see that no more tainted bread lay hidden within the abbey walls.

Satisfied that the danger there was contained, Agnes returned to her workroom with the loaf from Sister Margaret's table, prepared to begin the examination of the deadly herbs.

She turned to her small worktable, where she had placed the basket, but the basket of baneful plants was gone.

Sister Agnes – Death Comes to Godstow

Now beset by a deep foreboding, Sister Agnes felt the shadow of dread settle upon her. There was malice at work, of that she was certain. The basket of herbs held poison enough to sicken, perhaps even kill, the entire community of Godstow. Worse still, it had been under her care.

Just then, Isabel entered the workroom. Her brow creased as she took in Agnes's expression. "Sister, you are ill at ease. What troubles you still?"

Agnes exhaled sharply, pressing her lips into a thin line. "We have tended two of our sisters, both stricken by poison, yet I fear their afflictions were but the beginning. The basket of deadly herbs we gathered is gone, and I like not what this portends. I must take word to Mother Alice at once. She will be sore displeased at this course of events."

Without pause for announcement, Agnes entered the Abbess's chambers, gathering her resolve for what she must say.

Mother Alice looked up sharply, her expression one of impatience. "And what brings you here, Sister? Of late, you have taken to bursting into my chambers unbidden. What is it this time?"

Agnes inclined her head in brief apology but wasted no time. "It is grave news, Mother, most troubling indeed. Isabel and I went to the aid of two of our sisters, both taken ill by poison. Thanks be to God, we have treated them, and they rest peacefully now."

She drew a breath, pressing on. "Yet fearing there might be more such baneful plants within our walls, we searched the gardens. There we found two others besides the Fool's Parsley that struck down Sister Sophia. We gathered them into a basket and placed them where none should have found them. But when I returned from tending Sister Margaret, the basket was gone."

"How came the basket to be where another might so readily bear it away, Sister?" The abbess's tone was measured, but firm; the tightness of her lips betrayed her unease. Her patience, already frayed, wore thinner still. Yet beneath her stern façade, Mother Alice harbored a deeper fear—one she dared not voice. For the briefest moment, she considered sending for the undersheriff. But no, abbey matters must remain within abbey walls. Seeking aid from without was not yet an option.

"I set the basket upon a small worktable behind the great cabinet of herbs and potions, Mother. To hide it from prying eyes, I draped it with a length of white cloth. When I returned, the cloth lay on the floor, and the basket was gone."

The abbess's fingers tightened upon the arms of her chair. "We must find it, Sister—we must find the herbs."

"Aye, Mother. That be our task." And saying no more, Agnes turned and departed as swiftly as she had come.

As Agnes neared her workroom, Isabel came running, terror etched upon her face.

"Sister… there is another illness. But this one—this one is graver than the others."

Her breath came in sharp gasps, her weariness plain in her eyes, her body bent with fatigue.

Agnes steadied her. "Who this time, Isabel? And why say you she fares worse than the others?"

"It is Sister Ælfgifu. She is very old, three score and ten, and the novices must bear her from place to place. Two of them went to her chamber to fetch her for evening prayers, but they found her collapsed in her chair, her ale spilled upon the floor. Her breath is shallow, her rosary clutched tight in her frail fingers, her eyes wild. She claws at things unseen, crying out as if tormented. I fear she is dying, Sister—I am sore afraid. How came this curse upon Godstow?"

Agnes and Isabel entered Sister Ælfgifu's chamber in haste. The air was heavy with the scent of spilled ale, the cup overturned upon the rushes. The elderly nun was slumped in her chair, her breath shallow and uneven.

Agnes bent down and retrieved the cup, bringing it close to her nose. At once, she knew. Her expression darkened. "Deadly nightshade," she murmured. "We must work swiftly if she is to be saved. Isabel, go you at once—fetch the saltwater and mustard seed infusion."

Isabel turned and fled down the corridor, her feet swift upon the stone. Within moments, she returned, the emetic clutched in her hands. Agnes knelt beside Ælfgifu and pressed the cup to her lips.

"Come, dear sister. Drink."

But the old nun could not. Her parched tongue lay thick and useless in her mouth. A dry, rasping breath escaped her lips, and then her fingers curled inward, stiffening against her palms. A tremor passed through her, followed by a terrible convulsion. Her frail body arched, her back striking the wooden chair, her head knocking against the carved frame. Her breath came in one final, shuddering gasp—a terrible rattle in her throat—before all fell still.

The chamber lay steeped in silence. Agnes examined the old nun closely, searching in vain for a breath she knew she would not find. Slowly, she made the sign of the Cross over Ælfgifu's body and whispered a prayer for her soul.

Rising, she turned to those gathered. "She is gone. Our sister, called to her rest, now sits at the feet of our Savior."

A sob broke from Isabel's lips, and one of the novices stifled a cry. Agnes lingered but a moment longer, then turned and left the chamber, the sound of grief echoing in her wake.

With purposeful strides, Agnes made her way to the chapel, her heart heavy with sorrow and unease. The flickering glow of a single candle cast long shadows upon the worn stone floor as she knelt before the statue of the Blessed Virgin. Folding her hands tightly in prayer, she whispered aloud:

"O Blessed Mother, purest of women, what affliction has befallen our house? How have we, your humble servants, drawn such wrath upon us that our dear sister should leave us in such a grievous manner? What must we do to regain your favor and set right what is ill?"

The stillness of the chapel deepened, the silence thick as unspoken words. And then, as if carried on the breath of the night, a voice—soft as the rustling of veils, yet weighty with unseen power—stirred within Agnes's soul:

"You must seek the Enemy and cast him down. Only through steadfast faith and unceasing prayer shall you prevail. Your house depends upon it."

Agnes's breath caught in her throat. "But Holy Mother… how shall we seek the Enemy?"

No answer came. Only silence, vast and unyielding.

Yet beyond the hush of the sacred space, unseen in the shadows, two eyes, dark and cunning, watched her. A figure lingered in the dim recesses of the chapel, hidden where the candlelight did not reach.

The watcher's lips curled into a thin, knowing smile, a whisper slithering forth like the hiss of a serpent:

"You may seek, Sister… but you shall not find. Yet wait but a little while, and he shall find you."

Chapter 4
Misty Echoes of a Distant Past

In which rumours of demon worship begin to spread within Oxford town, causing unrest and fear among the townspeople. Lady Beatrix hears unsettling gossip and seeks Agnes's insight.

It began as any other day at Aylesbridge Manor. Lady Beatrix sat in her study, reviewing the manor's accounts, puzzling over the usual reckonings of charges and receipts, when her personal page burst into the chamber, breathless.

"My Lady… the groom bids me tell you there be ill rumours in Oxford town—whispers of devils and demons. He is sore troubled."

Lady Beatrix set down her quill and frowned. "And how came he by such news?"

Lady Beatrix – Osbert

"He rode to town to fetch forage for the horses, My Lady. The fields are near barren with the cold, and the beasts must eat."

Beatrix exhaled softly. "Very well. Bid him enter and tell me all."

The page bowed swiftly and was away. A short while later, he returned, with the manor's groom, Osbert the Horseman, at his heels.

Beatrix studied the man's face, weathered brow, and the way his hands twisted anxiously at the brim of his cap.

"Tell me, Osbert, what tidings trouble you so?"

The groom hesitated, shifting his weight. He cast a wary glance about the chamber, his voice little more than a whisper.

"My Lady, I beg you, do not press me to speak of such things. Words of devils and dark sorcery, cursed things upon the tongue. I dare not risk my soul."

"Folly, Osbert! Such talk holds no credence. They are but the ramblings of townsfolk, born of fear and ignorance. Pay them no heed."

"But, My Lady… there be them as swears they saw heathen rites under the midnight moon."

Beatrix shook her head. "Tales spun from shadows and dread. There is naught to it. Return to your beasts and let not such fancies weigh upon you further."

Osbert bowed, though his troubled visage lingered as he turned to go. As he departed, Beatrix bade her page accompany him and fetch her white palfrey. These rumours demanded a visit to the abbey and Sister Agnes.

As they returned to the stables, the page and the Master of the Horse spoke their fears in hushed tones. Above them, clouds scudded across the sky, veiling and unveiling the sun in restless motion. When its golden light broke through, it cast an eerie glow upon the fog settling in the low-lying fens, easing their disquiet a bit for but a moment. Yet, as the clouds returned, so too did their whispered dread.

"Master Osbert… these heathen rites trouble me greatly. What be they?"

"Hush, boy." The old groom cast a wary glance about him. "It be not known what such things may portend, and it be unwise to give them voice. Fell rites be wicked things, and ye risk more than ye know even to speak of them."

"But, Master Osbert… I would know of these things, that I might guard myself against them. If they be fell rites, surely our Lord and the Blessed Virgin shall keep me from harm."

"Boy, ye dare not stand 'twixt our Lord and the Prince of Darkness. To do so is folly, and surely ye shall perish—and with dire consequence."

"Yet still, Master Osbert, I would know."

As they walked, the sun slipped behind a veil of clouds, casting the world into shadow. Somewhere in the distance, a fox barked, the hunter seeking its prey. The boy clenched his eyes shut and murmured a prayer under his breath, his feet quick to follow the old ostler.

Lady Beatrix – Campfire

The page led Lady Beatrix's palfrey to the covered entryway of the manor house, where she stood ready, cloaked for the chill. Casting her gaze about, she sought her yeoman.

"Eadric, fetch you your horse and ride with me to the abbey. I needs must speak with Sister Agnes, and the carriage is too slow. I wish to make haste."

"Aye, My Lady. The groom leads my steed hither even now. We shall depart anon."

As soon as their mounts reached the entryway, they set out. Beatrix led, with Eadric close behind, his watchful eyes on both his mistress and the road ahead. They rode in steady silence for near half an hour when, ahead in the woods off the path, something caught Beatrix's eye, causing her to draw upon her reins.

Bringing her horse to a halt, her eyes narrowed at the sight of the scorched patch of earth in the woods hard by the road. The remains of a blackened pyre lay before her, its embers long cold, yet the stench of burnt flesh still clung to the air. Scattered among the ashes, fragments of bone appeared in the weak light. Dismounting, she stepped closer, drawing out her riding crop. Carefully, she prodded one of the charred remains with it, turning the bones gently.

"These are not the careless leavings of a hunter's fire, Eadric. This was deliberate. These are the remains of a ritual of some sort. Take you a cloth from your saddle pouches and gather some of these bones. Wrap them well, and we shall take them to Sister Agnes for her learned eye."

"Aye, My Lady.'Tis as good as done," and he stepped down from his horse. Taking a large piece of white linen from his saddle pouch, he selected the least burnt and damaged bones and wrapped them carefully before placing them gently in the pouch.

Sister Agnes – More Bones of the Innocent

"God give you good day, My Lady. What brings you to us?"

"Sister, I bear troubling news and a task that only you can undertake."

"What news troubles you so?"

"Sister Agnes, there are dire rumours in the town—whispers of devils, demons, and unholy rites. The townsfolk speak of strange fires burning upon a hill in the woods not far from Godstow. And as

I rode hither, I came upon what seemed a pyre. Within its charred remains, I found these bones. Eadric, give the good sister your bundle."

"Aye, My Lady. Sister, I have handled these as My Lady bade me. They are for your examination."

"Well then, let us see what grim tokens you have brought us. I shall need Isabel to aid in our work and write forth what we may find."

Beatrix turned to Eadric. "Eadric, go you to the outer workroom yonder and bid Isabel, the lay sister, bring her writing desk. She must record our findings. But step you no further than the outer workroom, for this is a house of nuns."

"Aye, My Lady. I shall do as you command."

As she had done oft ere this, Sister Agnes unwrapped the parcel with care, extracting the tiny bones one by one. She laid them upon her worktable and bade Isabel set to parchment all that she observed. Once she made her record, Agnes and Beatrix set themselves to the grim task of reassembling what they could of the remains.

"Many bones are missing, My Lady. Yet do you see these two skulls? There can be no doubt—at least two creatures lie here."

"Aye, Sister. And do you see these two backbones? Forsooth, I believe you speak true."

Painstakingly, the two women pieced together the frail remains, though the work was slow and many fragments lost. As Isabel took up her quill to sketch what lay before them, Agnes lifted her magnifying stone and bent closer to the fragile forms.

"My Lady, these are as before—newborn piglets. But see you here? The blade took their lives ere the fire. The blade took them not after death." Agnes traced the small nicks along the base of the skulls, then turned her glass to the tops of the backbones. "Look you at the wounds. The knife cut clean, severing flesh and bone alike. These were living sacrifices—slaughtered, then cast into the flames."

Isabel clasped her hands, her face pale. "I am sore afraid, Sister. Who could do such a wicked thing?"

Agnes exhaled sharply, her jaw set. "I know not, Isabel, but we needs must find out. And Mother will be wroth, I fear."

Without another word, Agnes turned and strode swiftly from the workroom, bound once more for a grim audience with the abbess.

Chapter 5
A Summoning by the Abbess

In which the abbess demands answers as gossip begins threatening the abbey's reputation. Isabel joins the investigation, and Alexis 'returns from the dead' to aid the team with her unique skills. She provides the first cryptic insights based on her keen observations of those within the abbey. Mother Superior becomes increasingly disturbed by events.

Before Sister Agnes had taken but ten steps from her workroom, a young novice came hurriedly round a corner, near colliding with her.

"Sister… Mother Superior bids you come to her anon, and she requires that you bring Isabel and the Lady Beatrix with you. She is sore vexed, Sister, and would have words with you at once."

Mother Alice – Demanding Answers

Agnes turned back to her workroom, where Beatrix and Isabel awaited her return from her errand to the abbess.

"Sister, you have been gone but a moment. Did you see Mother Alice?" Beatrix enquired.

"No, My Lady, I did not," Agnes replied, her face drawn with concern. "She sent my young novice to summon the three of us to her chambers."

Beatrix exchanged a glance with Isabel. "This bodes ill, Sister."

"Forsooth, My Lady, indeed, it does." Agnes exhaled, the weight of worry plain upon her face. "I fear she is provoked beyond her patience, and the tidings we bear will bring her little peace."

Stern-faced, the three strode toward the abbess's chamber. Mother Alice heard their footsteps upon the stone floor long ere she beheld them at her door.

"Well, Sister… what tidings bring you of this mischief that has befallen us? Speak plain, I pray, and spare me naught. I must know all."

"Mother,"—Agnes spoke with measured urgency— "we now hold it certain that a heathen sect is among us. We know not yet its full nature, nor the names of those who do partake in its wicked rites. Yet this much we know: they deal in blood sacrifice, and with the Feast of All Hallows nigh upon us, we fear that their wickedness shall grow, both in number and in foulness of deed.

"Lady Beatrix came upon the remnants of a profane fire while out riding. In the ashen remains, she found bones, which she has now brought before us for examination. Mother… they were piglets, even as before. Yet these, slain afore their bodies met the fire's embrace, were not the same as the earlier sacrifices."

"Sister, My Lady, Isabel—this assault upon our community has gone too far. The rumours spread through Oxford town as swiftly as the fire that consumed the piglets. Once loosed, such whispers are nigh impossible to silence."

Even as Mother Alice spoke, the young novice burst into the chamber, her face stricken with fear. She trembled as if the chill of the abbey walls had seeped into her young bones, her words stumbling from her lips.

"Sisters… Mother… there is a man without," she stammered, her breath coming in quick gasps. "His robes—they mark him as a man of high station. He demands… he demands an audience with you, Mother… and with you, Sister Agnes."

She scarce finished before a tall figure darkened the threshold, stepping into the chambers unbidden. Clad in the stark robes of a Dominican friar, he was a man of formidable presence—broad-shouldered, silver-gray hair, his face lined with purpose.

His long white tunic, bound at the waist with a simple belt, stood in stark contrast to the heavy black cappa that draped his form. With a slow, deliberate motion, he cast back his hood, revealing a tonsured pate.

His keen gaze swept the chamber, lingering on each woman in turn. The weight of the Church had arrived.

Then, in a voice that tolerated no contradiction, he spoke, addressing only Mother Alice.

"By order of His Holiness, Pope Boniface, Vicar of Christ and Supreme Pontiff, I am bid to speak with you at once regarding matters of grave concern to Holy Mother Church. I am his emissary, Friar Thomas de Glanville, a *Dominican inquisitor in disciplina*. (Inquisitor charged with matters of Church discipline.)

"Mother Alice de Gorges, this abbey stands at the pleasure of His Holiness. Should these whispers that have reached the ears of His Holiness bear truth, Holy Church may strip you of your charge, excommunicate you, and name you among the heretics."

A silence fell over the chamber, heavy as the stones that framed its walls.

Mother Alice's hands clenched at her sides, but her voice remained steady. "The Church would judge me a heretic? On what grounds, Friar? I have served God and Holy Mother Church with all obedience. Speak your accusations—all of them."

Friar Thomas inclined his head, his eyes unreadable. "I am sent not in haste, but in diligence. His Holiness bids me to uncover truth, not to cast judgment ere it be known. Yet be warned, Mother: should I find cause, Holy Church shall act without mercy."

Mother Alice – An Abbess's Resolve

Friar Thomas cast a hard, unforgiving gaze upon Mother Alice. His eyes swept over Sister Agnes, Isabel, and Lady Beatrix before returning to Agnes with a piercing look.

"And you, Sister?" His voice was low, edged with menace. "Are you numbered among those who conspire against Holy Church? Speak, and weigh your words well—for your future, your very soul, may hang upon them."

Before Agnes could draw breath to answer, Mother Alice's voice cut through the chamber.

"Friar Thomas, by what right do you question my nuns without leave?" Her tone was firm, unwavering. "Sister Agnes is our infirmarist, a healer both in body and spirit, and I shall not suffer you to cast doubt upon her devotion to God and Holy Mother Church."

The friar's lip curled. "Mother, I shall question whomsoever I choose, and howsoever I choose, in pursuit of truth. Think not to stand in my way. I am an emissary of His Holiness, and I shall root out the evil festering within these walls."

Mother Alice's eyes narrowed. "You speak as though judgment were already rendered. Upon what grounds do you level such accusations? As yet, you have uncovered naught but rumour."

Friar Thomas folded his arms across his chest. "God guides me, Mother, not you, a woman."

The abbess did not flinch. "There are rules, Friar. If I say you are unwelcome in this house of pious women, then you shall leave at once. The Church is clear upon this matter. If you doubt me, read well the *Rule of Saint Benedict*. As Mother Superior, I alone grant entry to men within these walls."

The friar's face darkened. "The *Rule* matters not. I act by the direct authority of His Holiness, and I shall do so as I see fit. Think not to hinder me with the words of a dead monk."

Mother Alice's eyes flashed. "Saint Benedict was a servant of God, Friar, and his *Rule* has guided Christ's faithful for centuries. Do you presume to stand above it?"

A long silence stretched between them. The friar's nostrils flared, his mouth a thin, unsmiling line.

"This matter is not ended, Mother," he declared, his tone heavy with warning. "The authority of His Holiness surpasses yours. See to your prayers, woman."

With a sharp turn, Friar Thomas swept from the room, his scribe hurrying at his heels. The frightened novice rushed to guide them back to the abbey gates, casting a furtive glance at Mother Alice before departing.

As the heavy door closed behind them, the abbess exhaled slowly, her jaw tight, her hands still clenched at her sides.

Sister Agnes – A Visitor in the Night

After the friar's departure, Agnes, Isabel, and Beatrix returned to Sister Agnes's workroom, their steps slow, their thoughts heavy. Not a word passed between them, yet each knew the same truth—all was not well.

Mother Alice had held her ground, yet Friar Thomas's warning lingered like the chill of a winter's breath. His parting words rang in their minds: the matter is not ended.

Within the workroom, Agnes broke the silence. "We must be certain, beyond all doubt, that our Godstow sisters are blameless in the eyes of Holy Church. If the friar seizes upon aught that seems amiss, he will carry word to Rome, and we—most of all, Mother Alice—shall pay dearly."

She exhaled sharply, her fingers pressing against the worn wood of the table. "We needs must ensure our purity, beyond question."

Before the others could reply, a sudden knock rapped against the workroom door. All three turned sharply.

The door creaked open, revealing the young novice who had led the friar from the abbey. Her earlier trembling was gone, though a shadow of unease still clung to her features.

"Sister," she said, dipping her head, "you have a visitor without. She says you will want to see her."

"Who be she?"

The novice shook her head. "I know not, Sister. She will not give her name, nor will she show her face. Her cloak is drawn tight, and her hood keeps her features in darkness.

A glance passed between Agnes, Beatrix, and Isabel.

Agnes squared her shoulders. "Bid her enter."

Their visitor appeared to be but a young girl, though her heavy cloak and deep hood cast her form in shadow, making it difficult to discern. When she spoke, her voice rasped, rough as wind through brittle reeds.

"Ken ye who I am, Sister? Ye should. Sure an' ye saved me life many a year past."

A sharp breath escaped Sister Agnes, her expression stricken with disbelief. "But it cannot be! You cannot be Alexis. We returned your form to your people when Mamo, your grandmother, bade us end our efforts to save you."

Her voice faltered as memories surfaced. "Mamo brought you to us, pleading for herbs and potions to heal the wound in your neck, the cruel work of an arbalest bolt. We did not expect you to live, and Mamo wished you to spend your last hours among your kin. I gave her all that I could, every draught and salve that might ease your suffering. Then, with the men of your family, she took you hence, back to your people. That was the last we heard of you, and in our hearts, we feared you lost to this world."

"Aye, Sister. But here I stand, and here shall I stay—to join your cause and repay you as I may for the life ye spared me."

Sister Agnes studied her, the flickering light casting long shadows across the worn stone floor. "Are you certain, Alexis? 'Tis no easy path we walk."

The girl straightened, her rasping voice firm. "Were I not certain, Sister, I would ne'er have darkened the abbey's gates. But certain I be, and certain shall I remain." The ghost of a knowing smile played upon her lips. "And think ye not to refuse me, for I have the sight. If I be welcome, I shall lend it, as best I can, to you and your sisters."

"You speak of our cause, Alexis. Forsooth, it has become a perilous one. The very life of our abbey's community, and most of all, Mother Superior…"

Agnes faltered, but ere she could go on, Alexis cut in. "Be at risk. Aye, Sister, well do I know it. There be mischief afoot—mischief of the basest kind, and the abbey stands at the heart of it."

Agnes sighed. "Rumours abound in the town, dark whispers of heresy, blasphemy, unholy rites, and…"

"And all point to Godstow." Alexis's voice was grim. "That, too, do I ken. Forget not, Sister, I have the sight. I know not yet who be the hand behind this mischief, but soon shall I uncover them — and soon shall you know.

"Even in the town there be those who claim to have seen strange fires burning in the night. And but this very day, Lady Beatrix came upon one such burning and within its foul remains did she find the bones of piglets—"

"Murdered in blood sacrifice." Alexis' voice dropped to a near whisper. "Aye, Sister, well I know it. I, too, have seen the fires. I have heard the chanting. Yet I dare not draw nigh. 'Twould be the end of me life to do so."

"Very well, Alexis. I shall entreat Mother to grant you leave to remain among us as a lay sister, for now. But mark me well, should this yoke prove too heavy for you to bear, you must speak of it anon."

Friar Thomas – Ominous Return

Alexis stood silent a moment, as though weighing her words. "Sister, I must tell you of something I beheld on my way hither. The novice who led me took no heed, but I both saw and heard. One among your companions, I fear, would cast her lot with The Enemy.

"As we passed, she spoke—but her words were not meant for the ears of any holy soul. I know not their meaning, but they rang foul upon the air. A friar clad in black and white, strong of frame and broad of shoulder, drew nigh as she spoke. He made no sign, yet his pace did slow, and I warrant he marked her words well."

Agnes's gaze sharpened. "Are you certain of what you saw, Alexis? Speak plainly. Do you speak of a vision, or be this truth seen with your own eyes?"

Alexis met her gaze, unwavering. "Sister, I saw with mine own eyes and heard with mine own ears. I had no need of the sight for this."

The heavy workroom door swung open, and there stood Friar Thomas, his gaze cold as a winter's dawn. "Sister, you will answer my queries truthfully, or you will be *interrogata sub tormentis* (questioned under torment)."

A chill settled over the chamber. Agnes stiffened, her fingers tightening at her sides. "You have no right, Friar. You must seek leave of Mother Alice. Such is the law of Holy Church."

The friar's lips curled in disdain. "Think not to school me in law, woman. I act by command of His Holiness, and I shall see his will done. Scribes! Take this obstinate nun to Castle Oxford and hold her fast. I shall come anon, and she shall speak plainly, else she shall answer for her dissembling."

At that moment, Mother Alice swept into the workroom, her stance rigid and unyielding, her novice cowering.

"Friar, release our sister. I have told you before—you shall not take her, nor question her, without my leave. And, Friar, you have not my leave even to set foot within these walls. Take your scribes and begone. I will not have this house of God disturbed by arrogance and threat.”

Never in all her years had Agnes heard Mother Alice speak thus. Vexed beyond patience, yet, Agnes suspected, still master of herself.

“I shall not release her, Mother, and I care not for your *Rule* nor that you are abbess. I shall carry out the directives of His Holiness, and no mere woman shall stay my hand.”

“But I shall.”

A hush fell over the chamber. In the doorway stood the Bishop of Lincoln, his robes still heavy with dust from his ride to Godstow from Rewley Abbey. His voice was quiet, yet it carried the weight of undeniable authority.

“Release the sister. Now.”

Chapter 6
A Light in the Woods

Wherein Friar Thomas and Bishop Oliver Sutton continue to clash over the friar's authority, and a nun spies a strange fire in the woods.

Friar Thomas looked up at the bishop, his expression darkening. "My Lord Bishop, do you not see that I act under the direct charge of His Holiness, sent to root out blasphemy within these walls? You can not hinder me, nor countermand the orders of the Holy Father."

Bishop Oliver Sutton met his gaze with steady resolve. "Oh, but I can, Friar. I shall convene an ecclesiastical court to weigh the charge and determine this nun's guilt or innocence. Until such a tribunal has rendered judgment, she is blameless in the eyes of Holy Church. Release her at once."

Bishop Sutton – A Friar's Defiance

"With all due respect to your station, my Lord Bishop, I shall not yield. And I am certain that His Holiness shall uphold my charge, no matter how strongly you and your company oppose it."

"Scribes, take the friar in hand and release the nun. Friar, do you seek imprisonment for defying my order? Mayhap I shall see to it, should you persist."

Silence reigned in the workroom. All eyes rested upon the friar, awaiting his reply. For his part, he stood rigid, his posture defiant, his eyes narrowed to slits, and his lips drawn in a thin, humorless line.

The bishop met his gaze, unwavering. When the friar gave no reply, Bishop Oliver Sutton let his voice cut through the stillness. "I require your answer forthwith, Friar. You have tried the patience of these sisters long enough. Speak now, and speak plainly."

Still, Friar Thomas refused to yield. He turned sharply, saying nothing, and wrenched himself free from the bishop's scribes. With stiff, deliberate strides, he quitted the workroom, his silence speaking volumes. The sisters, stunned by such brazen defiance, exchanged uneasy glances.

The bishop offered a slight smile, though his eyes remained grave. "Sisters, forsooth, I believe he shall trouble you no further—at least for now. But take heed. He will not abandon his hunt, nor his lust for heresy. And should he find what he seeks, the penalties will be most dire."

Gradually, the tension eased, though apprehension still lingered like a specter in the room. The bishop turned to Sister Agnes, his voice measured and calm.

"And now, Sister, I must away to Mother Superior's chambers, for we have much to discuss. Together, we must devise a strategy to safeguard this abbey and all who dwell within its walls. This friar seeks naught but the downfall of Godstow, and we must thwart him at all costs. Yet another peril looms—the sect you have uncovered, which endangers you still."

With a final, solemn nod, Bishop Oliver Sutton departed alongside Mother Alice, leaving Agnes and her companions to ponder the trials yet to come.

Mother Alice – A Plan to Save the Abbey

The bishop and the abbess walked purposefully toward her chambers. Once inside, they sat, and Mother Alice offered tea. The bishop, appearing weary from his exertions, accepted with the quiet grace of one accustomed to such courtesies, though he bore no air of entitlement. His demeanor set the tone for the conversation that followed.

"My Lord Bishop, your handling of this most trying matter was truly worthy of praise. It is very likely you have preserved the life of our sister, Agnes."

"It was my duty, Mother. My duty as bishop, as the friar's superior, and as a man. I could not stand by while Friar Thomas carried out his arrogant designs. Yet know this: we have bearded the lion, and we must prepare for the retaliation that shall surely follow."

"And how shall we prepare, My Lord?" Mother Alice's voice betrayed her concern, edged with both confusion and quiet despair. "If the friar appeals to His Holiness, I fear he shall receive whatever dispensation he desires, and there will be none who may dispute his word."

"There is a way, Mother," the bishop replied, his tone resolute. "I believe the friar will seek out the Bishop of Winchester, hoping he will countermand my authority. Winchester holds great sway in the highest circles of the clergy, and they regard his judgement as sound. But we shall move first and take our case directly to the Archbishop of Canterbury, the supreme head of the English Church. I know him well, and he will hear me. This will cut the friar off at that level and prevent him from advancing his cause unchecked. Yet we must act swiftly, for he will waste no time in his scheming."

Bishop Oliver rose slowly, his expression grave. "Mother, I shall send a messenger to the archbishop at once, entreating him to grant me an audience. My missive will outline our plight and urge him to withhold any judgment until we have spoken. I will request the earliest possible meeting and make haste for London at first light. I believe the archbishop presently resides at Lambeth Palace."

"Very well, My Lord." But despite her words, Mother Alice's voice held little confidence. "I shall pray for your success and your safe and swift return."

The bishop offered a faint smile as he gathered himself to depart. "Your prayers shall aid our cause, yet we must place our trust in the archbishop and his standing with His Holiness. God be with you, Mother Alice."

"And with you, My Lord Bishop."

With that, Bishop Oliver took his leave, returning to Rewley Abbey to take what rest he might before setting forth for London.

A few days after the bishop's departure, Friar Thomas and several of his scribes stormed Godstow's doors unbidden. This time, he did not wait for summons nor escort. The moment the young novice unbarred the great oaken doors, he strode in unchallenged.

"No need to lead me, child. I know well where I go. Mother Superior shall hear me, and this time she shall not deny me. Stand aside!"

Without awaiting permission, the friar thrust open the door to the abbess's chamber, the wood striking the stone wall with a resounding crash. He strode in, his scribes close behind, his face set like iron. Fixing Mother Alice with a cold glare, he spoke harshly.

"Mother, you will surrender to me the nun I seek, or I shall take both her and you to the dungeons of Castle Oxford forthwith. His Lordship of Winchester hath given full dispensation, and even now his messenger bears word of it to the archbishop. You have no choice in this matter, save to come quietly; you and your infirmarist."

He withdrew a parchment, marked with Winchester's seal, and held it forth.

"Read, if you must, and determine the truth of my words."

The abbess read:

Official Order from the Bishop of Winchester to Friar Thomas

"Given under our hand and seal in the twenty-ninth year of the reign of King Edward, by the grace of God, King of England, Lord of Ireland, and Duke of Aquitaine."

To Friar Thomas de Glanville, in disciplina, servant of Holy Mother Church and charged with the preservation of its purity, greetings in Christ.

Whereas there have arisen grievous reports of heresy and blasphemy within the Abbey of Godstow, touching upon matters most foul and contrary to the doctrine and discipline of Holy Church;

And whereas it is the solemn duty of the faithful to purge all corruption and ungodliness that may fester within the walls of Christ's houses, lest sin and sacrilege take hold among His chosen brides;

We, by virtue of our sacred office and with authority vested in us by Holy See, do hereby charge and empower thee, Friar Thomas, to proceed forthwith to the Abbey of Godstow, there to take into thy custody the Abbess, Alice de Gorges, and the nun called Sister Agnes, whom report names as having knowledge of these dire matters.

Thou shalt cause them to be conveyed to the royal gaol at Oxford Castle, where they shall be held in strict confinement until such time as they may be put to lawful questioning under ecclesiastical authority, that truth may be discerned and justice wrought.

And to this end, we do require the sheriff and his officers to render thee all aid in the carrying out of this most solemn charge.

Let no man hinder thee in this duty, lest he stand against the will of Holy Church and be counted among those who would abet heresy.

Given under our seal at Wolvesey Palace, this eighth day of October, in the year of Our Lord twelve hundred ninety-nine, and in the twenty-ninth year of the reign of our Sovereign Lord, Edward, King of England.

✠ John of Pontoise, by Divine Permission, Bishop of Winchester

Mother Alice blanched, but her voice remained firm.

"This is no lawful order, Friar. His Lordship of Winchester holds no authority within these walls. It is Lincoln to whom we owe obedience, and you cannot undo his command with a missive from another see. This is folly and presumption!"

Mother Alice's expression did not waver.

"What you do not know, Friar, is that His Lordship of Lincoln set forth days past to meet directly with His Grace the Archbishop. By now, he shall have received audience well before your messenger even nears him. The fate of your decree rests no longer in Winchester's hands, but with Canterbury himself, who may, at this very moment, be speaking with my Lord of Lincoln. It would be well for you to await the outcome. Should the Archbishop command it, we shall answer your questions — and gladly — but not before."

Her voice was quiet but unyielding, her countenance as unshaken as stone.

But the friar would not be deterred. His eyes burned with indignation. "Messenger or no, you will come, or we shall take you."

Mother Alice remained seated, her hands resting lightly upon the arms of her chair. "Remove me if you dare, Friar. Lay but a hand upon a woman of Holy Church, and you may not only forfeit your life but imperil your immortal soul."

For a moment, the friar hesitated, his jaw clenched in rage. Then, with a snarl, he tore the writ of Winchester from his belt and flung it onto the cold stone floor before her worktable. With a final scowl, he turned on his heel, his boots hammering the flagstones as he stormed out, his scribes scuttling after him.

Sister Margaret – A Fire in the Woods

Compline prayers and collation, a light repast of bread and cheese, now concluded, Sister Margaret felt a deep yearning for solitude. Her brush with death had left her more sobered than ever, and she longed for a moment of quiet reflection to offer thanks for God's mercy in sparing her life.

With steady purpose, she made her way to the bell tower, her habit whispering against the stone walls as she ascended the rugged wooden steps. Above her hung the great bell, its solemn peal reaching across Oxford town to call the faithful to prayer. One final climb remained, a short, narrow flight of steps leading to the trapdoor that opened onto the tower's roof.

Emerging into the crisp night air, Margaret knelt upon the worn stones, tilting her gaze heavenward. The firmament stretched above her, a vast canopy of shimmering stars, each a testament to the Almighty's boundless grace. Reverence filled her heart as she said a prayer of gratitude. God had spared her, and she knew that no measure of devotion, no length of vigil, could ever suffice to repay the debt she owed.

As Sister Margaret knelt in meditation, offering silent prayers of thanksgiving for her life spared, a flickering light caught her eye from the woods beyond the abbey walls. Her thoughts thus interrupted, she straightened, stretching stiff limbs and feeling the dull ache in her knees from the cold, hard stone. It was fitting, she thought, that she should suffer some small pain in penance, offering it up to the Almighty who had returned her to the land of the living.

Yet her gaze remained fixed on the distant light. It wavered, shifting with the wind, and soon she saw it for what it was, a fire burning in the depths of the forest. The night breeze, fresh and damp, carried a sound that chilled her to the bone — low voices, their murmur lilting and strange, as if in chant.

Alarm overtook her. This was no campfire of travelers nor the torch of a lost one seeking refuge. Heart pounding, she hurried to the trap door, wrenched it open, and fled down the narrow stairway. Once within the sheltering walls of the abbey, she nearly collided with Mother Alice, who walked the halls on her nightly rounds, ensuring all was well.

The abbess frowned, noting her pallor. "Sister, you are white as a winding sheet. What troubles you so?"

"Oh, Mother—there is something ill in the woods! I saw a fire burning where no fire should be, and the wind carried strange voices to my ears. I fear some wickedness is afoot!"

Chapter 7
A Novice's Guilt

In which Sister Agnes, Isabel, and Lady Beatrix seek the truth of the fire in the darkness, and a novice at the abbey acts suspiciously, spurring the investigation onward.

The night air carried a biting chill, and a stiff northern wind stirred the dry leaves, whispering through the trees. The three women, armed with torches, stepped beyond the abbey gates, their heavy woolen cloaks drawn tightly about them, hoods pulled low to shield their faces from the cold.

While Isabel and Lady Beatrix often carried out inquiries beyond the abbey walls, this night was different. Sister Agnes, who had long confined herself to the cloister and her workroom, had set aside her resolve, compelled by the urgency of what might lie ahead. Together, they looked for a path toward the place where Sister Margaret had spied the fire.

Upon a narrow deer track winding between the abbey grounds and the low rise of the wooded hills beyond, they paused. The damp earth bore the imprint of many feet, a path well-trodden by those who had passed that way before them.

Lady Beatrix – Who Were These Travelers?

Beatrix knelt in the grass beside the trail, running her fingers lightly over the pressed soil. "Sister, many have come this way—and of late," she murmured. "See here, the marks of common folk, their soles of rough leather worn thin. But look you closer—among them be the heavier tread of fine boots, such as only men of means may afford." She raised her gaze. "This gathering was no mere chance meeting, and, mark you, Sister, all who walked this path were men."

Sister Agnes knelt beside Beatrix at the edge of the grass, her cloak trailing in the dirt of the deer track. She ran her fingers lightly over the ground, studying the subtle indentations. "See here, My Lady… there be small holes in the earth beside the men's tracks. Though their number be unclear, for many footsteps lie atop one another, these marks tell a tale of their own. These were no common wayfarers. See how the holes run parallel to the prints, such as left by staffs, banners, or sacred symbols? But I misdoubt there be any here that bear the sign of our Lord."

Isabel, having ventured a short distance ahead, called out suddenly, her voice urgent. "Sister! My Lady! Come quickly! I have found where the fire Sister Margaret spied was burning!"

Taking care not to disturb the tracks, Agnes and Beatrix hastened after her, following the path until it widened into a clearing.

"Look you here," Isabel gestured to the ground. "The tracks separate here, forming a ring about the place where the fire burned."

Beatrix studied the earth, her eyes narrowing. "And mark you, Sister, one man, taller and broader than the rest, walked alone to the center. He bore some weight, that I can tell, for see how the prints sink deeper? And here," she pointed to a set of scuffed impressions, "he turns about widdershins at least twice… then halts, facing north —the place of darkness."

Agnes stepped to the center of the burned-out fire pit. "Here lies more of the same," she murmured grimly. "Piglet skeletons, I'll warrant. And there," she pointed along the charred remains, "see how another man's tracks lead from the circle to the fire? He paused, then turned back."

Isabel crouched, brushing ash from a section of disturbed ground. "Sister… My Lady… something heavy rested here. A large stone, mayhap? And see these furrows? 'Twas dragged upon poles to this place. What could this be?"

Agnes exhaled, her breath clouding in the chill air. "I know not, Isabel. But come morning light, we shall return and learn what we may. Bring your writing desk, the one you used in the abbey gardens, and take careful note of all we observe."

"Aye, Sister. I shall do as you ask."

The night wind freshened, cutting through the trees in icy gusts. The three women drew their cloaks tighter, the thick wool whipping about them as they braced against the cold.

"We must away," Agnes declared, casting a final glance at the circle of ashes. "The wind rises, and the northern breath of winter be upon us. We shall return after prayers and our morning meal."

She turned to Isabel. "Bring also the skeletons, that I may examine them more closely."

With that, the three turned back toward the abbey, their cloaks billowing in the rising wind, their minds heavy with foreboding.

Sister Agnes – The Morning After

Breakfast and prayers complete, Agnes and Isabel met Lady Beatrix at the previous night's discovery. The winds had lessened, and the pale sun made a feeble attempt to climb the heavens. With daylight now in their favor, the three women discerned many details, some more telling than others.

Sister Agnes knelt beside the charred remains of the fire. Scooping a handful of cold ash, she brought it to her nose and breathed deeply. Her expression darkened. "Sulfur. The stench of the Pit. These be no common pagans, but worshipers of The Adversary himself. Look, you—see the yellowed mounds amid the ashes? Sulfur, without doubt."

Isabel, drawing upon her five years of study under Agnes, made her own discovery. "Sister… this ash at the fire's edge bears a strange sweetness, much like the poisoned herbs we found in the chambers of the ailing sisters." She passed the ash to Agnes.

Agnes frowned as she sniffed the residue. "Isabel, you have made a grave discovery. These herbs, burnt in great quantity, would bring visions and stupor upon those who stood within the circle we beheld yestereve."

"There is more, Sister," said Lady Beatrix. "The great stone whose impression we glimpsed in the dark lies here, behind these bushes. See how it rests upon these dragging poles? And look, it is drenched in blood."

Agnes stepped forward, examining the thick, dried stains. Her voice dropped to a solemn whisper. "A sacrificial altar, My Lady."

Kneeling beside it, she ran her fingers over the dark crust of blood and rubbed it lightly between her fingertips. The texture flaked strangely. "This blood does not congeal as a man's humours would." Reaching into the pouch at her waist, she withdrew a length of fine linen and carefully pressed it to the stone, collecting the remnants. "We must test it further."

She rose and turned to her companions. "We have learned much, My Lady... Isabel. These rites be infernal in nature. This sect is a dire threat, not only to Godstow, but to Oxford town itself. We must away at once, that I may make certain of this blood."

Isabel dipped her quill and set the last strokes to her parchment. "Fear not, Sister, I have written all that we have seen and drawn the altar with its bloodied stains."

Agnes nodded. "Then let us not tarry."

Back in her workroom, Sister Agnes unfolded the linen cloth, revealing the dark stains of dried blood taken from the stone altar. With measured care, she scraped a small portion of the residue onto a clean shard of pottery. Then, taking up a candle, she brought the flame close, allowing the heat to char the sample. She leaned in and inhaled deeply.

"I discern no odor," she murmured. Her expression remained thoughtful as she turned to Isabel and Lady Beatrix. "Avicenna, in his *Canon of Medicine*, teaches that when we heat the humours of man thus, they give forth a foul stench. I, myself, have observed this when testing the humours of our afflicted sisters. Yet this sample yields no such corruption."

She set the pottery shard aside and reached for a clean vessel of warmed water. "Now, let us see how it fares in dissolution." She took another small scraping of the blood and sprinkled it into the water. The crimson flakes swirled, melting into the liquid almost at once. Agnes frowned in thought.

"Look, you—see how the blood dissolves without delay? The humours of man, when thus mixed, sink to the bottom and do not mingle so swiftly. This is not the blood of Christian flesh." She straightened, her voice certain. "It is the blood of beasts, perchance the piglets whose bones we found scattered in the fire pit."

Turning to the wooden tray upon her worktable, she lifted the small, brittle remains that she and her companions had gathered. Laying them gently beside the piglet bones Lady Beatrix had brought for comparison, Agnes studied them carefully using her magnifying stone.

Then she passed it to Beatrix so she might examine the injury more closely. Agnes met her gaze with a nod. "Now, I am certain. The blood sacrifice upon the stone altar was that of swine, not men. These be dangerous men, My Lady, given to animal sacrifice, heresy, and blasphemy."

Isabel – A Nervous Novice

Isabel left the workroom, her thoughts heavy. She sought solace in the abbey's chapel—a place of peace, where quiet meditation and prayers to the Blessed Virgin might ease the weight of the past days. The flickering glow of candlelight and torchlight lined the stone passageways, casting long shadows as she walked slowly through the cloister.

The stone arcade led from the workshop, passing alongside the abbey's gardens. It was open to the elements and supported by great, rounded arches of weathered limestone, with their sturdy pillars worn smooth by the passage of time. Above, the roof of overlapping slate tiles, hewn by hand, gleamed darkly in the dim light, cool with the dampness of the evening air.

Isabel entered through a wooden door bound in iron into the interior of the abbey and found herself at a crossing of passageways, where the cloister walk ran in a great square about the heart of the convent. Across from where she stood, the heavy oak doors of the chapel loomed, their surface carved with symbols of the Passion.

As she rounded the corner past the chapel, a flicker of movement in the dimness stopped her short. She drew back, then leaned carefully around the wall to glimpse what had startled her.

Half-hidden behind the great carved figure of Saint Peter, adjacent to the chapel's massive doors, stood one of the new novices —a slip of a girl, her form small and slight beneath the folds of her habit. Beside her, a small brazier smoldered, the scent of incense thick upon the air. Yet something about the scene was amiss.

The girl muttered low in a tongue unfamiliar to Isabel—words neither Latin nor any prayer spoken within these walls. She drew further into the shadows, listening intently as the novice continued her strange recitation. Isabel's breath stilled, and her heart quickened.

Then, the girl reached within her robe and drew forth a *Book of Hours*, her personal devotional, a thing of reverence meant for holy contemplation.

Lifting her face toward the brazier's wavering glow, she spoke again in that strange and unfamiliar tongue, the cadence ringing with an eerie reverence:

> *"Enaid goleuni, diflanna!*
> *Tyrd, dywyllwch du, galwant y meistri.*
> *Gair ofnadwy, gwana!*
> *Tân du, llynca'r geiriau, llynca'r goleuni!"*

> (Soul of light, vanish!
> Come, black darkness, the masters call.
> Dread word, weaken!
> Black fire, devour the words, devour the light!)

Isabel pressed herself deeper into the shadows, forcing herself to listen, forcing herself to remember every word. Something about the language—harsh, ancient, and almost frightening in its reverence—vexed her sorely.

Then, without hesitation, the girl tore several pages from the book and thrust them into the brazier.

The flames roared high, licking greedily at the parchment as a thick, black smoke curled upward. A foul, acrid stench filled the passage, cloying and heavy, unlike the sweet resins of the incense meant for holy devotion.

Isabel remained still as stone, watching, listening, waiting—until the novice, satisfied with her dark work, gathered her cloak close about her and slipped away, vanishing into the depths of the abbey.

In the shadows of the half-open chapel door, Isabel glimpsed another figure… also watching… waiting… listening.

Only when the novice was well beyond sight did Isabel dare to move. Her heart pounding, she turned on her heel and cast a quick glance toward the chapel door, now open, with no one in sight. Then she hurried back whence she came, her feet carrying her swiftly to Sister Agnes's workroom.

"Child, you are pale as death! What has befallen you?"

Sister Agnes's keen gaze fixed upon Isabel the moment she entered. The novice struggled to catch her breath, one hand pressed against her chest, her skin still clammy from fear.

"Oh, Sister… I have witnessed the most unholy thing within these abbey walls."

Agnes's face darkened. "Come now, Isabel. Sit down, take a breath, and tell me all."

Between gulps of air, Isabel recounted all she had seen—the novice's strange tongue, the cursed words, the burning of the sacred pages, the reek of blackened smoke. As she spoke, Agnes fetched quill and parchment, bidding Isabel to recall, as near as she might, the words she had heard.

Moments later, they both stared at the inked lines upon the page. Agnes's frown deepened. "We must take this to Mother Abbess at once. And beyond that, we must consult one whom I know who may bring us understanding."

Without delay, they made haste to Mother Alice's chambers.

Chapter 8
The Scholar's Insight

In which Sister Agnes and Lady Beatrix seek the wisdom of Professor Barrington on matters of sect practices, demon worship, and esoteric symbols. The mysterious chant the women heard reveals itself through the professor.

Agnes and Isabel entered Mother Alice's chambers. The abbess, taking note of their ashen faces and the weariness in their eyes, regarded them with grave concern. "You bring tidings that trouble you deeply — your faces speak of something most dire. Sit, take tea, and still your spirits, that I may hear all."

Isabel, breathless and shaken, struggled to find words, spilling forth a torrent of hurried speech, her thoughts tumbling over one another. Mother Alice's confusion was evident on her face. Seeing this, Agnes raised a hand to still Isabel's frantic attempt. "Hold, child. Take a deep breath and calm yourself, I shall tell the tale."

And so, Agnes began to set forth their grim account, her words steady, measured. Yet ere she could progress far, a knock came at the abbess's door, and from the dim-lit passage stepped Alexis, her cloak and hood drawn close about her.

Alexis – A Hidden Witness

"Alexis… what brings you here at this hour?"

"I have seen much, Mother. I have seen and heard what Isabel has seen and heard—mayhap with different eyes and ears."

"Sit, take some tea, and speak freely, Alexis."

As she spoke, Sister Agnes moved to a small worktable in the abbess's chambers and there took up quill and parchment, ready to set down the tale Alexis would tell.

"Take heed, Mother, I have the sight. And the sight reveals all that lies hidden within a soul when I cast mine eyes upon them. The novice I beheld was working a spell of dark magic. Well do I know the words she uttered:

> *Enaid goleuni, diflanna!*
> *Tyrd, dywyllwch du, galwant y meistri.*
> *Gair ofnadwy, gwana!*
> *Tân du, llynca'r geiriau, llynca'r goleuni!*

"I know not its meaning, but I ken full well that it is evil."

As Alexis spoke, Isabel gasped. "She did tear pages from a book, Sister! I saw it with mine own eyes."

"Aye, that she did," Alexis confirmed. "And as she chanted her spell, she did cast those pages into the fire."

"Her *Book of Hours*," Isabel whispered, horror-stricken.

"Aye, that was the one," Alexis said, her voice low. "She tore them from the binding and flung them into the fire, and the flames leapt high, nearly to the rafters. And the stench, Sister, it wasn't parchment alone. I swear it carried the reek of the pit itself. When the novice had finished her spell, she fled, and Isabel and I did the same, though we took different paths, each of us seeking ye, Mother, to bring this tale."

"You bring us a tale most strange and troubling, Alexis. Sight or no, your eyes watched keenly, and your ears missed naught. Your memory serves you well, recalling all that passed before you.

"Had not both you and Isabel borne witness, I would scarce believe such grievous acts from one of our own. But verily, you saw and heard, and your words match hers as one voice."

Sister Agnes turned to the abbess. "Mother, I have weighed their words well, and they be as you say, true beyond doubt. What they portend, we know not, yet certain it is that evil of the basest kind moves in our midst. If I may counsel you, Mother, we should seek the wisdom of Professor Barrington, for he knows well the cunning of the enemy and the means by which he threatens Holy Church."

Mother Alice inclined her head. "And so shall it be, Sister. Alexis, on the morrow at first light, you shall go with all speed to the college and entreat the professor to come hither. Tell him the matter is of grave import and brooks no delay."

"Aye, Mother, that shall I do, and with all speed."

Unseen by the gathered company, concealed within the shadows of the outer entry, a novice listened, her breath scarce more than a whisper in the still air. She had heard all. Now she need only decide how best to carry word to her master.

Her opportunity soon revealed itself. A young scullery maid, her labours done for the day, made her way to the outer gate, bound for the town. The novice followed in silence.

Professor Barrington – Visit From a Scholar

Professor Barrington entered Mother Alice's chambers with quiet dignity. "Mother, it is ever an honor to see you, though I perceive a weight upon your spirit. What trouble has compelled you to summon me with such urgency?"

"Professor, your coming so swiftly is a grace we did not expect. I would not have summoned you but that our need is grave and your wisdom sorely required."

"Well then, Mother, let us waste no words. Pray, sit, and share what you know."

Mother Alice inclined her head and turned toward Alexis, who stood nearby, her expression grave. "I know well that Alexis, our lay sister, can best recount the matter that has set our house in turmoil. She has seen with her own eyes that which we cannot fathom, and she shall give you such details as she may. Then, good Professor, I beseech you—help us make sense of this horror, that we may discern how to combat it."

She drew a steadying breath before continuing. "As you surely know, the rise of a sect given to the veneration of dark forces troubles us. They have already spilled the blood of beasts upon unholy altars, and we fear it shall not end there. The townsfolk grow fearful, and with them, an *inquisitor in disciplina* has taken it upon himself to persecute us as though we were the very root of the evil. Worse still, what Alexis and Isabel witnessed this past eve, within the very walls of our sacred cloister, gives me the greatest pause. One of our own—one sworn to God's service—committed acts most grievous, as though in league with The Adversary himself."

Her voice was tight with sorrow. "We needs must know what this portends. Is she deceived? Bewitched? Or does she act with full knowledge of the evil she serves? Professor, we must understand, ere it is too late."

As she had with Mother Alice, Alexis recounted her tale for the professor in great detail. When she came to the incantation, she closed her eyes, as if summoning the memory from the depths of her mind, and recited it aloud:

> *Enaid goleuni, diflanna!*
> *Tyrd, dywyllwch du, galwant y meistri.*
> *Gair ofnadwy, gwana!*
> *Tân du, llynca'r geiriau, llynca'r goleuni!*

The professor raised a hand, halting her speech. A shadow passed over his face. "That is dire indeed," he said gravely. "I know this tongue—it is Brythonic Celtic, an ancient language, long used in rites of power. It is common in sects that serve dark forces."

He paused, then translated in a voice edged with unease:

> *Soul of light, vanish!*
> *Come, black darkness, the masters call.*
> *Dread word, weaken!*
> *Black fire, devour the words, devour the light!*

A sharp gasp escaped Isabel, her hands tightening into fists.

Alexis exhaled sharply, her voice low and urgent. "She has called The Adversary into our cloister. This is a defilement... an abomination." She turned to the professor. "What power have we to guard against such evil, when even the walls of our sanctuary have been breached?"

"Without knowing it, you have summoned evil into your very midst. This novice you speak of has likely long trafficked with the darkness. The sect that now plagues you believes itself heir to the Druids of old—those heathen priests who practiced dark rites of blood and shadow long ere the coming of Our Savior. The ancient Romans sought to stamp them out, and Holy Church has ever condemned their practices as blasphemy. Yet here, even now, their dark rites are reborn."

He paused, meeting Mother Alice's eyes before continuing, his voice weighted with a cautioning tone. "They are cunning folk, adept at deceit, and clever in masking their purpose. By subtlety and stealth, they recruit from among good Christian souls, swelling their ranks in secrecy."

Mother Alice sat silent, staring fixedly into the candle's flicker, clearly shaken. At last, she spoke softly, "Then how may we discern these blasphemers, good Professor? One novice has shown herself plainly to Isabel and Alexis, yet we cannot know how many more may lurk unseen within these walls."

Mother Alice and the Professor – Beginnings of a Plan

"There is but one way, Mother," he said reluctantly. "You must watch your sisters closely—note well their comings and goings, observe their deeds, their speech. The young and impressionable they seek first, yet some elder sisters, even if strong in mind and body, may also accept their ways. Only those weak with age or illness would they likely shun."

"I like not the thought of spying upon my sisters, Professor," Mother Alice replied quietly. "Yet if needs must, needs must."

It was Alexis who spoke next, her voice soft, reluctant, almost a whisper. "Mother, this I can do. I've the skill to watch without being seen, and to listen without being heard. Will you have me take on this unpleasant burden?"

"A burden it is indeed, child," Mother Alice answered gently, yet with quiet authority. "But you know the urgency of protecting our sisters, our cloistered community, and Holy Church herself. Therefore, I do charge you with this task. But mark this well: we must undertake it in utmost secrecy. Were word of it to spread, it would sorely trouble the hearts of our sisters."

"Aye, Mother. That I ken too well. My heart, too, is sorely troubled." Quietly, with her head bowed, Alexis departed Mother Alice's chambers, uttering no further word, her thoughts bent sorrowfully upon her mission.

BOOK THE SECOND
MORE DISTURBING CLUES

As the clues pile up, the missing novice returns to Godstow and leaves again, returning this time to *The Kindred,* where she meets her fate.

Chapter 9
A Clue Among the Trees

In which we uncover evidence of a sinister gathering on Boar's Hill, suggesting the sect's activities may be escalating.

Within the abbey walls of Godstow, the community observed the Feast of Saint Michael and All Angels with prayers and reverent celebrations. Saint Michael, Archangel and protector, was honored as a sign of Heaven's triumph over darkness.

But scarcely had a few days passed ere anxious whispers from Oxford town reached the cloister. Townsfolk arrived with disturbing tales, recounting a profane gathering—a blasphemous mockery of Michaelmas, conducted by unknown persons deep within the shadowed woods. The reports spoke of eerie chanting and dark revelry, twisted echoes of sacred rites.

**Sister Agnes and Lady Beatrix –
a Mockery of Saint Michael**

Troubled, the sisters listened, sensing an unseen threat drawing nigh. Sister Agnes, alongside Isabel and Lady Beatrix, soon learned more. Villagers whispered of a vile parody of their holy feast, carried out in secret under cover of night on Boar's Hill.

Seeking evidence, Lady Beatrix accompanied Agnes and Isabel to the place described, guided discreetly by anxious townsfolk. Amidst scattered leaves and scorched earth, she beheld the remnants of unholy rites. At the center lay the blackened embers of another sacrilegious fire, and around it, signs of feasting and revelry that mocked the holy day just passed.

Beatrix knelt, brushing cold ash from her fingers, disturbed deeply. "They defile our holy days," she murmured softly. "Look. Look at these bones—an animal sacrifice, or from its form, mayhap a child or a small man, intended as mockery."

"That be no child, My Lady. Those bones be those of a beast, but we needs must examine them closely in my workroom."

Lady Beatrix nodded grimly and summoned Isabel closer. "Mark this well, Isabel. This was no random merrymaking. This was deliberate blasphemy, a dark mimicry of Saint Michael's triumph over evil."

Isabel, her voice faltering, looked anxiously toward the wood's edge. "Sister, what evil rises thus? Why mock the holy archangel?"

Agnes drew a breath to steady herself. "To mock Saint Michael is to mock the victory of Heaven itself. These blasphemers grow bold, and their purpose is plain. I fear this profane feast is but a prelude, and greater wickedness awaits." Silently, they rose and, with Beatrix's stable hand accompanying them, brought the charred bones to Agnes's workroom. They returned to the abbey in wordless procession, each weighed down by troubled thoughts of what darkness might yet unfold.

Sister Agnes – A Strange Sacrifice

When they arrived back at the abbey, Alexis awaited them in Sister Agnes's workroom. Ere the stable hand could set the strange bones upon the worktable, Alexis hastened forward with troubling tidings.

"Sister, My Lady, Isabel, I bear disturbing news from the town. Sir Geoffrey de Harcourt, Baron of Cumnor, hath summoned the undersheriff. It seems the baron's menagerie has suffered theft—a rare beast is gone missing."

Agnes regarded the charred bones now laid carefully before her, their form oddly human yet not. After a long pause, she spoke softly, but with certainty. "This be no human nor plain beast of field or forest. I believe that this creature is a monkey—a Barbary macaque from the shores of North Africa, brought hence by knights returning from distant lands. Oft are these creatures kept as curiosities by noblemen of means."

She cast a sorrowful glance at her companions. "Mark you well, such an animal is rare and costly, a sign indeed of the wealth and cunning of those we face. Our foes grow bolder and ever more brazen."

Lady Beatrix met Agnes's grave gaze. "Then Sir Geoffrey's creature has met a terrible fate, Sister, for it disappeared from his menagerie but a short time past. It would seem their evil grows bolder day by day."

Agnes nodded gravely. "Then swiftly must we act, for darker deeds surely lie before us. Come, let us examine the beast more closely." She reached for her magnifying stone and bent to study the charred remains with careful attention. "Isabel, fetch your writing tools and parchment, that you may set down all we observe."

"Aye, Sister. At once." Isabel hurried to gather her writing implements.

Lady Beatrix stepped nearer to the worktable, studying the bones thoughtfully. Her expression darkened as she spoke. "Look closely, Sister… there be clear signs of a blade upon the creature's neck."

Agnes leaned forward, nodding solemnly. "Verily, My Lady. The poor beast did feel the sharp bite of a knife ere the flames consumed it. And further, observe the blue discoloration upon lips and tongue. Such marks speak plain of poison."

She straightened slowly, her face troubled. It seems the sect did test their draught upon the creature ere striking the mortal blow. Mayhap they now prepare themselves for greater evil yet, trying their craft upon larger beasts, learning thus how best to perform a sacrifice of human life." Agnes's voice lowered with grim certainty. "If such be their intent, we needs must look to Samhain—the heathen feast of wandering spirits, which falls beside our own Feast of All Hallows. Methinks 'tis then they mean to make a human offering."

Chapter 10

A Missing Novice

In which the disappearance of a novice causes unrest within the abbey. Mother Superior's fears intensify, and the stakes for Agnes and her friends increase. Agnes returns to her garden seeking more clues.

Shortly after their troubling discoveries following the Feast of Saint Michael, Agnes, Beatrix, Isabel, and Alexis gathered in Mother Alice's chamber for tea.

"I am sorely troubled," Mother Alice began, her voice heavy with anxiety, a manner most unlike her usually composed demeanor. "The cruel sacrificing of innocent beasts, the blasphemy committed against the Feast of Saint Michael, and now this fearful possibility—a human sacrifice planned for Samhain, the eve of All Saints—fills my heart with dread."

Sister Agnes, deeply unsettled by their lack of progress in unmasking the sect, spoke quietly but resolutely. "Mother, we do all that lies within our power, yet it seems little enough. I, too, am sore vexed at our inability to delve deeper into the workings of this unholy gathering. We strive in earnest to uncover the identities of those who serve The Adversary, but beyond their substantial resources and influence, we know lamentably little."

Mother Alice sighed softly, meeting Agnes's troubled gaze. "Then let us redouble our vigilance. Our foes move secretly and swiftly; we must likewise be watchful, patient, and wise, lest their darkness overtake us."

Alexis – A Disruption in Her Mission

The following morning, after the sisters had broken their fast on bread and cheese, pottage, and ale, Alexis came breathless into Agnes's workroom. This morn had been special indeed—a merchant from the town had brought fresh fruit, a rare delicacy seldom seen at the abbey. The sisters had savored it silently as the Mother Abbess read aloud from the Old Testament.

"Sister Agnes! I am sore confused. I have followed the novice suspected of blasphemy without fail. Yet now I can find her nowhere. I fear she may have fled the abbey, but when I questioned the novice who attends the gate, she did swear unto me that none have passed in or out since last evening. Also, I have learned her name: Cecily Fuller. She is daughter to a wealthy family of wool merchants and cloth processors. I heard tell her kin sent her hither, for she was wild of spirit and did consort overmuch with the young men of the town."

"This bodes ill, Alexis. This Cecily Fuller has every reason to join with The Adversary. If she is wild of spirit, she will not likely see the danger in which she places herself. And, if she is weak for young men, she easily could succumb to the advances of one. We needs must find her before she comes to grave harm."

"Many of my clan camp nearby. I shall go to them and beg their help. May I leave the abbey on this errand, Sister?"

"You may go. Go with God and with my blessing upon you."

"Thank you, Sister. I shall find this Cecily and bring her back or know wherein she hides." And Alexis was away in a trice.

Alexis – Cecily Found and Cecily Lost

It took Alexis but little time to reach the place where her family had made camp. Seeking out her grandfather, she spoke to him of the matter concerning Cecily Fuller.

"Well do I ken the Fuller clan," he mused. "They be fine folk and have shown us many a kindness. Aye, and 'tis time we gave back what they once gave us, by finding their wayward lass."

Alexis leaned in, her voice low. "Then, Grandfather, do you and our kin know where to begin this search? Forsooth, the sisters whisper that she is a fey child… and mayhap they speak true."

"We shall begin in the town, Granddaughter. There, in the taverns, we shall hear word of her. A wild young lass who seeks commerce with the men of the town will not pass unnoticed. There, mayhap, we shall learn whither she has gone."

Alexis returned to the abbey, and but two days hence, a message arrived from her grandfather:

> *Granddaughter, come to our camp. We have news*
> *for you.*

Wasting no time, Alexis made haste to her family's encampment and sought out her grandfather.

"You know the old, empty manor house at the edge of Oxford town, where men whisper that the Templars once met in days long past?"

"Aye, Grandfather. Well do I know that place. 'Tis a house of ill reputation, haunted, so folk say, by wicked spirits. Many a tale speaks of vile deeds done within its walls."

"'Tis there you'll find your wayward girl. God speed you on your quest."

"Many thanks to you and our kin for this knowledge. I'll seek Lady Beatrix, and together we'll find this blasphemer and bring her back to the abbey — so we may learn what we must about The Adversary."

In the company of her cousin and his pony cart, Alexis made haste to the manor of Lady Beatrix. As they arrived, she dismounted swiftly and rapped upon the great oaken door, its iron fittings cold beneath her hand. A bitter wind swept round the corners of the house, seeping through her cloak and hood. She shivered and wished, not for the first time, that she wore a nun's habit beneath her cloak, for its thick wool would have served better against such chill.

The door opened with a creak, and Beatrix's footman regarded her with a dubious eye. "Aye, and who be ye, waif? We give naught to beggars at the portal. If ye seek charity, go ye round to the kitchen, where the servants mayhap have a crust of bread for the likes of ye."

Alexis squared her shoulders. "Nay, Footman. Tell My Lady that Alexis of Godstow begs urgent audience with her. I have no time to tarry."

The footman hesitated but, at length, turned and vanished within. Soon, Lady Beatrix herself appeared upon the threshold, her expression marked by curiosity. "Alexis! What trouble brings you all this way to find me?"

"The novice I spoke of, the one who performed profane acts outside the chapel, has vanished from the abbey. We fear she is in league with The Adversary and his followers. My grandfather sought word of her and found she now dwells in the old manor house where folk say the Templars once did meet in times long past. We must go there, My Lady, and take her back to the abbey that we may learn what she knows of the followers."

Beatrix regarded her gravely, considering the weight of her words. At length, she gave a solemn nod. "Child, you may send your cousin back to his encampment. I shall take you in my own pony cart."

Turning, she called to her footman. "Fetch the groom and have him ready my cart at once. Then shall you drive us to the old Templar house."

"Aye, My Lady. At once."

Within moments, the groom arrived, guiding the pony cart to the manor's entrance. Beatrix and Alexis climbed within, and the groom took his place upon the driver's seat. Wrapped in warm blankets embroidered with the arms of the de Aylesbridge family, the two women set forth toward the old Templar house, the wind sharp at their backs.

Upon reaching their destination, the women and Beatrix's footman alighted and made their way to the forsaken dwelling. The door, though thick and weathered, had rotted in places, and the burly footman made short work of forcing it ajar.

Led by the footman, the women moved cautiously through the vast house, seeking hidden passages and priest's holes where the novice might have concealed herself. Yet they found none. The place stood empty. As they entered a great chamber, a former banqueting hall with a large hearth at its end, Alexis called out:

"My Lady! Come quick and have a look. The ashes in the grate, do you see? They're fresh."

Beatrix knelt by the fireplace, sifting through the remains. "Forsooth, Alexis. These ashes are unlike the old ones scattered about this house. Mark you, the newer ones be of green, wet wood, gathered nearby, still damp with the rains of recent weeks. The rest, dry and well-burnt, are from a time long gone. Someone kindled this fire but a few days past. Cecily has been here -- and fled ere we came."

"Now must we take up our search anew, My Lady." Alexis murmured, "For I fear darker truths lie ahead."

Alexis and Lady Beatrix – Mother Alice's Fears

With heavy hearts, Alexis and Beatrix returned to the abbey and sought Mother Alice. They found her in her chambers, pacing, her hands clasped, clearly awaiting news of their errand.

"What say you, child? Did you find the novice called Cecily Fuller?"

Beatrix hesitated ere she answered. "Nay, Mother. We discovered her hiding place, the old Templar house, yet she was gone ere we arrived, the fire in the banqueting hall kindled but shortly before."

Mother Alice's countenance darkened. "Certes, this is grievous news. She consorted with The Adversary — of that I am now sure. This bodes ill. A heavy dread weighs upon me for our house, and the townsfolk tremble. Rumors pass from mouth to mouth, and each day more souls gather at our doors, begging sanctuary. We needs must find this wayward novice — and swiftly — lest terror take root both within these walls and without."

Sister Agnes – More Clues in the Garden

Agnes was sore vexed. That the novice could flee the abbey without trace was troubling enough, but that none had marked her passing was yet more disturbing. She pulled her heavy cloak close against the chill and made her way to the gardens.

Mayhap a clue had escaped her notice. As she trod the narrow pathways between the beds, her gaze fell upon something amiss.

"Now what have we here?" she murmured, stopping short.

Upon the damp earth lay the imprint of a small foot -- the mark of a turnshoe; soft leather, the common wear of nuns and novices alike. The footprint was slight, belonging to none but a young girl.

Agnes cast her gaze about. Naught stirred, and the prints vanished into the gravel path beyond, and left no trace of whither they turned or fled. A frown creased her brow.

Yet not beyond the reach of Mother Alice's worries, Cecily Fuller still lay hidden within the abbey walls — concealed among hay and shadows of the stable near the gardens.

Chapter 11
The Hidden Relic

 *In which a disturbing find in the woods presents new and dark possibilities, as well as a veiled threat to those who probe too deeply. Professor Barrington investigates.*

Cecily fled the abbey through a door, known only to a few nuns and novices, that allowed unseen passage beyond the walls of the abbey grounds. So rapidly had she left the entry to the chapel that she wore only her novice's white habit. Once outside the abbey walls, the biting cold made her wish for her warm, heavy cloak. But Cecily Fuller had a task to perform. She must get word to the leader of her sect of blasphemers that she had, indeed, offered her sacred Book of Hours as a sacrifice to the old gods. Then, she needs must return to the abbey unseen.

On the crest of a low hill in a field at the estate of a wealthy benefactor of The Sect, she met with one of her apostate brethren. "I bring good tidings, brother. I have made an offering to the old gods of my *Book of Hours*. And, forsooth, I offered it right outside the doors of Godstow's chapel!"

"Fool! Were you seen?"

She pondered a moment. "Nay… or at least, I think not. And even had they heard, they would not have understood my prayer, for I spoke it in the old tongue."

"Our leader will not be pleased, Sister. He wishes you to spy upon your sister nuns that he may overtake Godstow in the names of the Old Ones. But you risked discovery. I must away to forewarn him that we may be near found out. Now take you back to Godstow and pray to the Old Ones that you were invisible to anyone nigh to your place of sacrifice."

Shocked and sorely disappointed by her brother's rebuke, Cecily fled the hilltop and made haste for the abbey. Slipping back into the abbey grounds through the hidden passage was easy enough. But once within, she sought both shelter from the cold and a place to hide in secret until the sisters had taken to their rest and she might steal back to her cell unseen.

Casting about in the gardens, with their high stalks of plants withering with the coming winter cold, she spied a hay barn connected to the stable where the nuns kept but two workhorses to draw the wagons to and from Oxford town. The shed, tucked behind the stable and half-hidden out of sight from the cloisters and the kitchens, offered a perfect place to hide. Formed of three rough-planked walls, it was open to the elements, but Cecily knew that she could find shelter in the piles of hay. Inside, the shed was quiet save for the low shuffling of a horse in a nearby stall in the stable. The air was warmer inside, still and thick with the scent of hay and old wood.

Fearing discovery by one of the sisters, Cecily cowered beneath the loose hay piled in the barn, the stiff, sharp stalks tearing at her habit and grazing her fair skin. Now, troubled and afraid, she wondered how she might undo the harm already wrought within the convent walls.

She believed it possible that someone heard her whispering her prayers to the Old Ones, her voice a thin thread between worlds. Mayhap someone even had spied her casting her *Book of Hours* into the flames. And she knew with a creeping dread that chilled her more than the autumn air, that if *The Kindred* learned of her treachery, if she dared confess her sin of consorting with them, she herself would become a sacrifice. *The Kindred* was a sect of blasphemers that worshiped The Adversary openly. They, intolerant of betrayers, certainly would mete out the harshest punishment of all.

Agnes, Beatrix, and Isabel came to learn of *The Kindred*— a secretive band sworn in dark devotion to the Adversary. Though made up mostly of men, a few hard-edged women counted among their number. They claimed descent from the Druids of old. Their leader, called only the High Sacrificer, was a name spoken in dread — a shadow ever feared.

None could claim to have laid eyes upon him, nor did any know his true name. To some, he was no mere mortal, but a demon loosed from the Pit, come to rain misery upon the abbeys and upon Oxford town. To others, he was a man of flesh and blood — perhaps a merchant of great wealth, one who walked among the godly by day, yet by night, beneath the shroud of midnight, donned his mantle as the master of *The Kindred*.

Others whispered of a darker truth — that he was of noble blood, a man who had lived beyond the years of mortal men, one whom Death itself could not claim.

Whispers of *The Kindred* and their dread leader reached Beatrix's ears as she pursued her inquiries into the foul sacrifices of beasts. The tales varied, but in each was a thread of terror, and a warning unspoken: to seek *The Kindred* was to tread the path of death.

Cecily – Confrontation in the Hay Barn

Cecily stilled her breath beneath the hay, ears straining. A footstep upon the wooden planks. Someone was within the shed.

The steps drew closer.

She peered out from her nest of hay, heart hammering. There, not three feet away, stood the stable hand—the young, strapping man charged with tending the heavy work unfit for the sisters. Cecily suspected that he was of *The Kindred* and, like her, sent to spy upon the sisters.

"I know ye be here, Cecily," came the quiet, knowing voice. "Show yourself, or I shall find ye." She pressed herself tighter into the hay, willing herself into silence. The foul scent of sweat clung to him, thick and sour, turning her belly. A day's toil left him in sore need of cleansing.

"Very well then," he murmured, stepping forward, boots rustling against the hay. "I am coming in."

With measured patience, he kicked aside the loose hay, knowing she had nowhere to flee. And at last, trembling, Cecily emerged— pale, habit in tatters, recoiling into the shadows as his gaze fell upon her.

A wicked smile curled upon his lips, part amusement, part something darker. "So, my girl… ye have broken the convent's rules, and now ye would break from *The Kindred*? Well do I know of your intent to return to the abbey. You have broken the convent's rules by joining *The Kindred*. Ahh, yes, my pretty miss. I know all for have I not eyes and ears of my own within these abbey walls? Tell me—do ye ken what the High Sacrificer shall do when he learns of your treachery?"

She swallowed hard, her breath coming in short, fearful gasps.

"But…" he mused, stepping closer, "mayhap I can help ye."

Cecily needed not ask his price.

Oft had she seen that look in a man's eyes, and she knew full well what he would demand in exchange for his silence. And, to save herself, she braced herself to yield to it.

He closed the distance, reaching for her arm.

But ere he could lay hands upon her, a voice rang out from beyond the shed.

"Martin!" It was one of the elder sisters, keeper of the stable. "Where are you, lad?"

Martin stiffened, head snapping toward the open wall of the shed. Cecily dared not move.

"I am here, Sister!" he called, voice smooth, as though he bore nothing to hide. Stepping out of the shed, he rounded its corner to where the old nun stood, shielding Cecily from her sight. "I was only fetching hay for the horses."

The nun's tone was firm. "See that you finish your labours and be gone ere the evening bell."

"Aye, Sister. That shall I do."

He turned back, slipping around the side of the shed to re-enter, expecting to claim his prize. But in that fleeting moment of distraction, Cecily, creeping silently around the far corner, was gone.

Cecily – Discovered

After slipping away from the stable, Cecily sought refuge in a small work shed near the gardens. Her garments were torn, her stomach empty, and her body chilled to the bone by the cutting wind. She shivered as she ducked inside, desperate to escape not only the bitter cold but also Martin, the stable hand.

Yet ere she could settle within, a voice, calm yet firm, rooted her to the spot. "So, you have returned to us, Cecily." The novice froze. She knew that voice at once—Sister Agnes.

"Aye, Sister. That I have," Cecily murmured, her voice scarcely above a whisper.

Agnes stepped forward, her keen gaze taking in the girl's wretched state. "You are nigh frozen, child. Attend me at once, and I shall fetch you warm garments and hot soup."

Without further protest, Cecily followed the nun into the darkened cloister, moving silently as the wind howled beyond the abbey walls. Once within Agnes's workroom, the nun moved quickly, wrapping Cecily in a heavy woolen cloak and setting a steaming bowl of thick pottage before her.

As Cecily ate, Agnes seated herself beside the fire, her hands folded in her lap. "Now, tell me, child, of your wanderings. Well do we know that you have consorted with *The Kindred.* Are you of their number?"

Cecily hesitated, her fingers tightening around the wooden spoon. At last, she exhaled and nodded. "Mayhap, Sister. But forsooth, I fear them greatly. They have promised me much if I would but join them, if I would spy upon my sisters within the abbey. But I have gone too far. I sorely fear the High Sacrificer when he learns that I have spoken of this."

Agnes leaned forward, her voice calm but unyielding. "And who, Cecily, is this High Sacrificer?"

The girl shook her head. "None know, Sister. He is the leader of *The Kindred,* the one who wields the blade to sacrifice unto the Old Ones. But none have seen his face."

Agnes studied her for a long moment, then spoke with quiet authority. "Get you to your chamber, Cecily, and there shall you remain for now. On the morrow, after prayers and the breaking of our fast, you shall see Mother Alice. I shall have a lay sister bring you bread and water in the morning. Meanwhile, content yourself with prayer to the Holy Mother and beg her intercession for the safety of your soul."

Cecily swallowed hard and bowed her head. "Aye, Sister." She rose, the heavy cloak again gathered tightly about her, and slipped from the workroom. As the door closed behind her, Agnes remained by the fire, her thoughts dark and troubled.

Sister Agnes – Mother Superior

Come morning, it didn't take Sister Agnes long to recount the tale of the wayward novice. "I don't believe, Mother, that Cecily merits our trust. She does not belong in our community."

"But to release her outside the cloister, Sister, tempts her to rejoin *The Kindred*. At least within these walls, we can observe her and obtain what we needs must know about *The Kindred*."

As Agnes and Mother Alice spoke, a lay sister arrived with Cecily.

"What have you done, child?" A sharp, stern edge punctuated the abbess's speech. "You have consorted with The Adversary, and you have broken your vows as a novice. You know how grave is your sin. It is not for me to hear your confession or assign penance. That shall the confessor do with you on the morrow. However, I can remove you as a novice and assign you the duties of a lay sister, and that role shall you have for as long as the confessor deems. When you return to your chamber, you shall remove your novice's habit and assume the rough tunic of a lay sister. Sister Agnes will assign such work tasks as needs may be. Now, take you from my sight and repair to your chamber. Await Sister Agnes's instructions."

Head held low, hiding the resentment in her eyes, Cecily left the abbess's chambers and, in the company of the lay sister, went to her chamber to await her duties and her confession on the morrow.

Lady Beatrix – A Strange Find in the Woods

Mounting her white rouncey mare, Lady Beatrix set forth toward the abbey.

Her rouncey was a fine beast, bred in noble stables, loyal, obedient, and even-tempered, as befitted a lady of high station. Whenever she chose to ride, rather than take her pony cart or carriage, it was always this steed she favored.

This day, however, as she rode the path near the place of the sacrificial fire, she reined her horse to a halt. Something on the ground caught her eye. Dismounting, she dropped the reins, trusting the horse to wait as she stepped lightly toward the clearing. The horse, obedient to her mistress, nibbled grass and waited patiently for Beatrix to return.

The fire pit lay cold. But near its edge, something strange lay in a nest of rotting leaves. She knelt, brushing away the damp foliage. A stone it was, worn and broken, yet upon its surface, markings unlike any she had seen.

"Forsooth, this is no common stone…" she whispered to herself.

Retrieving her saddlebag, she wrapped the fragments carefully and secured them. Swinging into the saddle, she urged her mount into a smooth canter.

Straight for the abbey. Straight to Sister Agnes.

Professor Barrington – The Stone

Sister Agnes turned the stone over in her hands, tracing the rough, jagged edges.

"This is no common rock, My Lady. Look you at these carvings. I know not their meaning."

Beatrix nodded. "We must summon the professor. Mayhap he can tell us what this portends."

Agnes called for a lay sister. "Go you to Balliol and fetch Professor Barrington. Tell him there is a matter of grave import he must examine. Bid him make haste and say that I have sent you."

The sister gave a quick nod and departed, her footsteps fading into the cloister.

In the stillness that followed, time seemed to stretch. Agnes and Beatrix sat unmoving and silent, eyes fixed on the doorway, listening to every distant sound.

At last, the lay sister returned, breathless and wide-eyed, and behind her came Professor Barrington, his jaw tight with concern.

"What have you for me this time, Sister? My Lady?"

Both women spoke at once. "This stone."

Agnes stepped forward, "See you these markings? They seem of no tongue I know."

Professor Barrington frowned, leaning closer. "You are correct, Sister. These are runes, ancient symbols of the Elder Futhark alphabet, used by Germanic tribes ere the eighth century."

Dipping his quill, he carefully transcribed the symbols onto parchment.

ÞM ᛋFᚲRIᚹIᚲM Iᛋ ᚲHᛟᛋMᚾ.
ÞM ᚷᛟᛗᛋ ᛗMᛗFᚾᛗ Bᛚᛟᛟᛗ ᚹᛟR Bᛚᛟᛟᛗ.
ᛏᚢRᚾ BFᚲᚲ ᚹRᛟM ᛉᛟᚢR ᛃᚢMᛋᛏ ᛟR ᛋᚢᚹᚹMR ᛗMFᚦ.

After a long pause, he translated aloud:

*"The sacrifice is chosen.
The gods demand blood for blood.
Turn back from your quest or suffer death."*

Agnes exchanged a troubled glance with Beatrix.

The professor exhaled, his voice grave.

"This is no relic of the past. It is newly made, though fashioned to appear old. And it is a stern warning. If you continue upon this path, Sister… you will tread a road most perilous."

Chapter 12
Echoes of Sacrifice

In which we observe the unearthing of the truth behind the animal sacrifices and the reality of a missing novice presumed dead.

Cecily repaired to her chamber as bidden, but her heart was full of bitterness. She felt ensnared, caught fast betwixt *The Kindred* and Holy Church, and most grievously, beneath the ever-watchful eye of the nuns at Godstow. Yet in truth, she bore no love for the abbey, nor felt any true tie to it. Her parents had sent her hither but to be rid of her, that they might wash their hands of the trouble she brought.

By her reckoning, she owed naught to the sisters within these walls. She could depart at will… could she not?

But if she fled, what then? What would the High Sacrificer—called by the sect the Archdruid—say? Nay, what would he do? The thought chilled her to the marrow. She knew well the price of betrayal.

She needed aid. But to whom could she turn? Her thoughts wandered to Martin. He was of *The Kindred,* of that, she was sure. Mayhap he would help her. If she could reach him before Sister Agnes sent her to her labours… if he would but aid her escape…

Worse yet loomed her confession on the morrow. What words could she offer that would not damn her soul further still?

Cecily – The Dread of Confession

Cecily tossed upon her straw-stuffed mattress, the weight of penance pressing heavy upon her. The confessor, though oft kindly in manner, was a man of strict discipline, and when need arose, he spared not the rod.

A fast, perhaps— days without food, or weeks on naught but bread and water. Or she might stand in vigil all the night long, chanting prayers without rest. Most dreaded of all, she feared being barefoot to walk the cloister garth, or worse, the full circuit of the abbey's outer walls, murmuring prayers of repentance.

And such would not excuse her from her Aves or her Pater Nosters. Nay, she must do all these, and more.

With dawn's first light came the lay sister, bearing her a humble repast: a crust of bread, a bruised apple, and a cup of cold water. She stood silently by as Cecily ate, then cast a glance toward the high window, where the sun's rays crept o'er the stone sill.

"The sun begins its ascent," she said at last. "Come. We must go to the chapel. The confessor awaits you."

Cecily – The Confessor

To Cecily, it seemed as though the very world had stilled, turning its collective gaze upon her to see what she would do next.

The confessor, an elderly priest from Rewley Abbey, regarded her carefully.

"Well, my child, whence comest thou, and to what end?"

The confessor spoke in the old language of the Church, his words laced with the familiar thee and thou. In addition, he used the Latin form of the sacred confession.

Taking a deep breath, Cecily began—praying silently that her Latin, such as it was, would not fail her. She had resolved, still fearing for her immortal soul, to confess all she had done, trusting in the mercy of the confessor… and in his discretion.

> Confiteor Deo omnipotenti, et beatae Mariae Virgini,
> et omnibus sanctis eius, et tibi, pater, quia peccavi nimis.
> *(I confess to Almighty God, to the Blessed Virgin Mary,*
> *to all His saints, and to you, Father, that I have sinned*
> *exceedingly.)*

> Sum nequam, mulier nequissima, et inimica mihi
> ipsi.
> *(I am wicked, a most wicked woman, and hostile to my*
> *own self.)*

> Confiteor Deo, et dominae meae sanctae Mariae, et
> omnibus sanctis, et tibi, domine sacerdos, peccata quae
> ab ultima confessione mea feci.
> *(I confess to God, and to my Lady Saint Mary, and to all*
> *the saints, and to you, Lord Priest, the sins which I have*
> *committed since my last confession.)*

> Cum daemonibus consociata sum, et cum eis qui
> cum daemonibus consociantur.
> *(I have consorted with demons, and with those who*
> *consort with demons.)*

> Sorores meas moniales et hanc abbatiam prodidi,
> sciens plene quid facerem et quid sequeretur.

(I have betrayed my sister nuns and this abbey, fully knowing what I did and what would follow.)

Ritus impios peregi, cum Adversario communicavi intra muros huius abbatiae, sacras eius claustras polluens.
(I have conducted vile rites, communicated with The Adversary within the walls of this abbey, defiling its sacred cloisters.)

Et peto absolutionem a te, et sanam poenitentiam pro peccatis meis.
(And I ask absolution from you, and healing penance for my sins.)

Et peto absolutionem a Deo, a beata Maria Virgine, et ab omnibus sanctis.
(And I ask absolution from God, from the Blessed Virgin Mary, and from all the saints.)

The confessor was silent, contemplating all that he had heard. This was a mortal sin, perhaps the gravest. It merited a penance commensurate with its peril not only to Cecily but to her sisters and to the abbey itself.

When the confessor finally spoke, his voice held neither rage nor pity. It was calm and resolute, firm but not cruel, and wholly in keeping with his stern reputation.

"Cecily Fuller, thou hast opened thy heart, thy mind, and thy soul to The Adversary. There is no graver sin. More grievous still, thou hast placed thy sisters in jeopardy by performing vile rites within these sacred cloisters.

"I might call for excommunication—or even death by fire. Yet our Lord is a merciful Lord, and I entrust thee now to His justice and His mercy. But know this: our Lord giveth not without requiring something in return. If thou wouldst seek redemption, thou must render unto Him thy suffering.

"Therefore, thou shalt fast, taking naught but bread and water for forty days and forty nights. Thou shalt sleep upon the stone floor, wrapped only in sackcloth, and without the comfort of fire.

"At Matins, Lauds, and Vespers, thou shalt prostrate thyself in the chapel and confess thy sins before the sisters. Yet none shall answer thy prayers.

"Each night, thou shalt walk the cloister yard barefoot, without any covering upon thy feet. When the bell tolls for Compline, thou shalt kneel before the altar until the last candle doth gutter.

"Daily, thou shalt recite the Seven Penitential Psalms, and fifteen Aves and fifteen Paternosters.

"From this moment, thou art a lay sister—neither novice nor nun, but a servant of this house. Thou shalt speak only with Sister Agnes or with Mother Alice. No laughter shall be thine, nor comfort, nor ease, until Holy Church doth lift thy burden."

Cecily trembled. *Holy Church lift the burden?* Nay—it was a burden beyond bearing. Her resolve hardened. No matter the risk, she would escape this place and return to *The Kindred*.

Cecily – Planning Her Escape

The young lay sister led Cecily back to her chamber, now more prison than cell. But to Cecily's surprise, once the door shut, the girl turned to her.

"You are of *The Kindred*."

It was not a question.

"I can help you leave this place—if that be your wish."

Cecily stared. "Is this some cunning? Can you truly help me escape?"

"I can take you to one who will see you safely beyond these walls, back to your people. They will be eager to hear all that you have learned."

Cecily hesitated. Perhaps it was a snare laid for her. Yet it was the only path open to her.

"Who is this savior? I would know the name of the one in whose hands I place my life."

"Martin—the stable hand."

Cecily's blood turned to ice. "Oh, no... Is there no other? What of you?"

"Sister Agnes soon would miss me. Even now, I risk much."

Cecily swallowed. "Very well. How shall I meet with Martin?"

"After the bell for Compline, I shall lead you to the hidden passage. Martin shall await you there, and he will take you to the Archdruid. But do not tarry—he dare not be caught."

Cecily sighed, her eyes staring at the rough floor of her chamber. "I shall be ready when you come."

Cecily – Fleeing Godstow

The lay sister arrived at Cecily's chamber just as the Compline bell tolled. Together, she and Cecily headed for the secret passage. Cecily opened the gate, slowly, carefully, fearing but knowing what awaited her on the other side.

Nor was she disappointed. There stood Martin, clad in a rough-spun tunic damp with sweat.

"Well, little girl. I see ye've come to me at last as I knew ye would."

"Take me to the Archdruid. Now… please…" she pleaded, fearing what would come next.

"Nay, lassie. Not before I've had my due."

He stepped toward her, hand outstretched. She backed away, trying to evade his grasp, but to no avail. Martin seized her roughly and yanked her close. She prayed he would either grow weary and let her go or take his due and be done with her.

She let her body go limp, like a rag doll—but Martin paid no heed to her stillness. Instead, he only grew more brutal, leaving Cecily no choice but to endure his assault. When at last he finished, he stepped back, leaving her bruised, her pale skin chafed raw by the coarse scrape of his beard. She braced for him to begin again, but he did not. He only stared, as though admiring his handiwork.

"Well, me girl… ye did well. Mayhap we'll enjoy each other again, soon."

Cecily prayed with all that remained in her that such a day would never come.

Cecily – The Archdruid

In the woods nigh to the spot where the fire pit had burned, celebrating unholy rites, the Archdruid, also known as the High Sacrificer, awaited Cecily and Martin.

"So, Martin… you have returned our lost lamb to us. Very good. I am well pleased." The Archdruid stepped toward Cecily, studying her closely. "Martin, my boy, she bears signs of mistreatment. Haven't I warned you about that? Ye treat a lady like a lady, not like some common harlot. Cecily is to be royalty. She shall reign as a queen. I may even grant her the honor of making a sacrifice to the Old Ones. Imagine, Martin, a squealing piglet on our sacrificial altar. One of the women present feeds the piglet the purple draught, and the piglet goes limp. Cecily will take the sacrificial blade from my hand and cut the creature's throat as I did with the others. Or, mayhap, it won't be a piglet on Samhain… the Old Ones deserve more. Much more. We shall see, shan't we, Cecily?"

Martin's grin deepened as he laughed softly to himself, already understanding the Archdruid's intent.

Chapter 13
The Unholy Sacrifice

In which The Kindred's ritual leads to a horrifying climax, and the nuns discover a novice still is missing. Sister Agnes and her team face the gruesome reality of The Kindred's actions. The abbey's community becomes more agitated as another novice describes sacrifices such as that of Cecily.

In a chamber lit only by tallow candles and the flickering glow of a brazier, the Archdruid conferred with his astrologer.

"When," he asked, "is the hour most propitious for the sacrifice? We must rend the veil that lies between the world of the living and the realm of the dead. The offering must not go amiss."

The astrologer was old and wise, his silver-white hair hanging past his shoulders. A circlet of gold, etched with strange astrological symbols, rested upon his brow. His robe was adorned with stars and planets, shimmering faintly in the lamplight. He bowed low, fingers tracing the symbols inked upon a vellum chart.

The Archdruid – The Astrologer

"My Lord Archdruid," he began, his voice soft and bearing the weight of confidence born of his long life among the stars and planets, "Friday—Samhain—is most auspicious. All the planets of import lie gathered in Scorpio.

"In the 5th planetary hour, from the third quarter to the midnight toll, Saturn holds sway: he is the lord of death, of endings, of time, and of the underworld. It is then we must consecrate the circle and summon forth the spirits. Then shall we prepare the novice for her sacred journey unto the altar."

He raised his eyes. "In the 7th hour, from the second watch of the new day, Mars shall rule. The red planet, lord of blood, power, and sacrifice, shall rule from the heart of Scorpio. It is then the blade must fall."

The Archdruid gave a slow nod.

"She must be prepared in the old manner." The Archdruid picked up the instruction. "First, she shall be robed in black, naked beneath its folds, and upon her brow shall be bound the sacred mistletoe, pleasing to the Old Ones. Her hands shall be fastened before her— bear no shackles, only binding—for she must walk of her own will. Before she walks to the high altar, she shall drink of the sacred wine, mixed with henbane and other herbs known to gladden the spirits. I shall speak words unto her: that she, crowned queen of *The Kindred* and hailed as the hope of our people in the eyes of the Old Ones, will live among the gods."

He smiled, but there was no joy, only solemnity, in it.

"I shall walk her to the altar. There, a white robe shall be placed upon her — a symbol of her purity, and necessary to the Old Ones. Her black robe will be taken and burned in the sacred flames of the sacrificial fire. Then I shall set a circlet of gold upon her brow.

"She will then recline upon the stone, hands unbound, and lost in dreams, seeing visions of glory and gods, ere sleep takes her. The chants of the Company shall rise—hymns to the Old Ones—and she, lifted in ecstasy, drifts between the worlds."

He drew in a long breath and continued.

"When the moon is high, I shall raise the blade. In the tenth hour, when Mars is strongest, I shall strike. Her essence shall show the way to our salvation. You, brother astrologer, shall catch her humours in the sacred black obsidian bowl, that we may scry the path ahead."

The astrologer bowed again.

"So mote it be, my Lord Archdruid."

The High Sacrificer – Samhain Ritual Sacrifice Interrupted

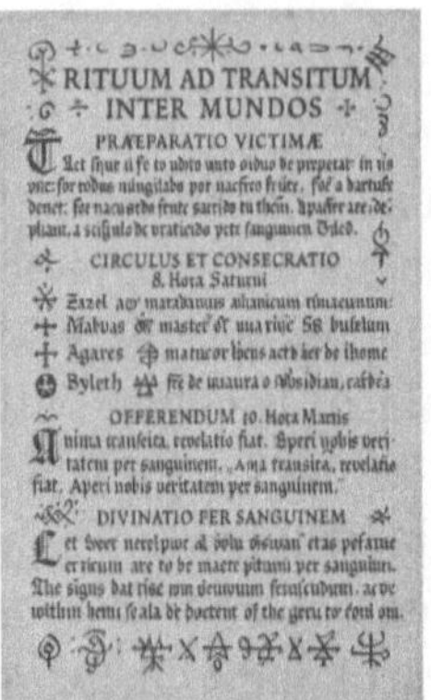

The astrologer whispered to the Archdruid, "My lord, the hour for the ritual fast approaches. We needs must prepare the novice for her marriage to the Old Ones. Here is the ancient script that shows us the way."

Reading from the *Codex Obscura*, the grimoire of *The Kindred*, the astrologer intoned the instructions for the *Ritual of the Veil*.

In the 5th hour, when Saturn reigns over the dark heavens:

Prepare the place with salt and ash.
Mark the circle with the sign of the Cross inverted
and the Seal of the Serpent.
Let no light touch its heart but the flame of
blackened wax.
Cast the herbs of night into the fire: henbane,
mandrake, belladonna.
Anoint the vessel of obsidian with oil of myrrh and
blood of the cock.
Let the novice be clothed in black, her flesh bare
beneath, and mistletoe encircling her brow.
Let her drink of the red wine thrice blessed in the
name of the Lord of the Pit.
Whisper to her: "Thou art the chosen bride, queen

of the Old Ones, and thine offering shall open the gate."

In the 7th hour, when Mars burns above in Scorpio*:*

Lead her forth in silence.
Exchange her robe for white and set the circlet of gold upon her head.
Place her upon the stone. Let the chanting begin: "Sanguis pro sanguine. Lux cedat. Aperite portas mortuorum."
(Blood for blood. Let the light yield. Open the gates of the dead.)
Let the blade be obsidian, washed in wine and ash.
At the stroke of the hour, pierce the throat, and catch the blood in the sacred bowl.
Hold the bowl to the flame, and gaze deep.
Let the shadows speak their truths, and the dead reveal what is to come.

Thus is the veil sundered. Thus are the Old Ones fed. Thus, shall their favor descend.

The Archdruid, now the High Sacrificer, pulled his robes about him—black woolen cloth with a cowl, secured at the waist by a cord of human hair. Upon his face he wore a bronze mask depicting a skull. At his hip hung a small obsidian amulet etched with the sigil of *The Kindred,* and upon his hands he wore red gloves, signifying the blood shed. He walked barefoot.

The High Sacrificer called for two of his acolytes. "Come ye and prepare the novice Cecily for her ascent to the Old Ones."

Two guardsmen departed for the chamber wherein the novice waited. They clothed her naked body in a robe of deepest black.

The High Sacrificer continued, "She will stand before the Old Ones bare, with her deepest secrets exposed to their sight."

Woven into her hair, the acolytes placed sprigs of mistletoe, and they bound her hands before her with a cord spun under the waning moon.

One of the acolytes brought a chalice of the wine of sight, a sweet red wine mingled with henbane, vervain, and the sap of ash. Looking about her, as the wine captured her mind, she called out to the acolytes, "Take me at once to the sacred circle wherein I may take my rightful place as the Queen of *The Kindred*. For I see the Old Ones and they beckon me to their dark presence."

The men bade her wait but a moment more while the sacred circle, prepared for her presence, cast its magic. Whispering to her, one of the acolytes said, "You are the chosen bride, crowned queen of the Old Ones, and it is your offering that shall open the gate."

"Then convey me there at once that I may begin my reign!"

Following the instructions in the *Codex*, two further acolytes prepared the circle of salt and ash. With the smoke of yew and cypress ascending heavenward, the High Sacrificer entered the sacred circle and intoned the unholy names:

> "**Zazel** *(Spirit of Saturn, Gatekeeper of the Dead)*
> **Marbas** *(Revealer of Secrets)*
> **Agares** *(Master of tongues and portents)*
> **Byleth** *(He who governs sacrifice and offerings)*"

The two acolytes brought Cecily to the edge of the circle where the High Sacrificer took her by her hand and walked her to the center near the high altar of stone. There he gently removed her robe of black and, turning her slowly around that all might see, called out to the Old Ones, "Look upon us, O ancient gods of *The Kindred*, and you spirits of our Druids, long since gathered to your august number.

"We bring you Cecily, a novice nun, pure in heart and body as our offering to you that you might take her as your bride and queen."

The assembled company solemnly intoned, "So mote it be."

The High Sacrificer then replaced her black robe with a robe of purest white. "This robe of white, O Ancient Ones, symbolizes your bride's purity of mind, body, and spirit." Again, he turned her around, now three times that the company might gaze upon her. He placed a golden circlet, engraved with the terrible names of the demons of the Pit, upon her brow.

"Behold her, O Ancient Ones, and receive her into thy dread presence. By the sacred names of Astaroth and Samael, hidden princes of the Pit, I conjure thee!"

"So mote it be." The Company then chanted,

"Sanguis pro sanguine. Lux cedat. Aperite portas mortuorum.
(Blood for blood. Let the light yield. Open the gates of the dead)

Sanguis pro sanguine. Lux cedat. Aperite portas mortuorum.

Sanguis pro sanguine. Lux cedat. Aperite portas mortuorum.

Sanguis pro sanguine. Lux cedat. Aperite portas mortuorum.

Sanguis pro sanguine. Lux cedat. Aperite portas mortuorum. "

The High Sacrificer led her with solemn care to the altar and loosed her bindings.

"Is it the hour when Mars resides in Scorpio?"

"It is, my Lord High Sacrificer."

"We offer flesh for flesh, breath for breath, blood for blood. O ye watchers in shadow, receive her whom we send. Open unto us the gates of that which lies beyond. Thus is the veil sundered. Thus are the Old Ones fed. Thus, shall their favor descend."

At that moment, screams and howls rang out from the surrounding woods, as though all the demons of the Pit had risen to earth for the Samhain revels. The astrologer and the High Sacrificer froze in place, confusion writ upon their faces.

But these were no cries from Hell—they came from the Pope's own guards, an armed company stationed in secret over the past month in Oxford and held in concealment until this very hour. At their head rode Friar Thomas, sword drawn and fire in his eyes.

"What devilry is this?" the High Sacrificer cried. "Who comes unbidden into this holy place?"

"I am Friar Thomas, a servant of the Inquisition, and I, with my righteous company, have come to put an end to your blasphemy and prevent the murder of this innocent girl."

The High Sacrificer recoiled at the words. Then, with a swirl of his robes and a hissed curse, he fled the altar and swiftly vanished into the trees. *The Kindred* broke apart in confusion and fear, their chants dissolving into cries as the Pope's soldiers surged forward, giving chase through wood and shadow.

Friar Thomas – The Rescue

Friar Thomas strode to the altar and lifted the novice, dazed and shivering, from the cold stone. As he raised her into his arms, clouds swept across the moon's bright face, casting the glade into sudden darkness. Thunder growled low in the heavens, and rain fell in earnest, heavy and unrelenting.

Just as the friar reached his mount, a towering coal-black destrier, sixteen hands high with a mane like falling night, a bolt of lightning clove the altar in twain with a roar like the rending of the very firmament.

With the aid of a soldier, Thomas hoisted the near-unconscious Cecily behind him. Then, with a cry to his men, he struck his heels to the destrier's flanks, and they thundered through the storm, bound for the safety of the abbey.

Lady Beatrix – The Missing Novice

The lay sister entered Agnes's workroom, her face pale with unease. "Sister, when I went to take Cecily her morning meal to break her fast, she was not in her chamber. I have searched every place I could think of, but I found her not. What can have befallen her?"

"I know not," Agnes replied gravely, "but we must search again. I shall fetch Isabel, and the three of us shall make haste."

After a thorough search, the women found no trace of the novice. Fearing the worst, Agnes and Isabel went at once to Mother Alice.

"Mother," Agnes began, "this morning the lay sister charged with Cecily's care brought tidings most strange. When she brought the morning meal, the girl was not in her chamber. Together we searched the abbey, but to no avail, and the hour is becoming late."

Mother Alice frowned. "Surely, she passed through the main gate. Did the sister at the portal see her?"

"Nay, Mother. She did not."

"Then she must yet be within these walls."

Agnes shook her head. "Mother, I fear she may have escaped through the hidden passage. A few among us know of it… and we must suppose Cecily did also."

"Then send word to Lady Beatrix. Let us widen our search beyond the cloister walls."

Agnes turned to the lay sister. "Find someone swift of foot to carry a message to Lady Beatrix. Tell her that Mother Alice, with the greatest urgency, bids her search beyond the abbey walls — into the town if needs be — for any sign of Cecily. Then she is to return at once with word of what she learns. And make haste. I fear the worst."

They had a long wait. The days crept by with no word, each one stretching longer than the last. Though their duties kept them occupied by day, Agnes and Mother Alice found their thoughts ever turning to Cecily. By the third evening, the burden of uncertainty pressed sorely upon them, and they took to keeping vigil as the sun sank low and shadows lengthened. About them, the abbey grew still —the last of the sisters retiring, doors drawn to with quiet care. Yet still, they waited, cloaked in uneasy silence.

The news, when at last it came, came not from Lady Beatrix. Late though the hour was, a novice—dispatched by the sister on watch at the gate—burst into Agnes's workroom, breathless.

"Mother Alice! Sister Agnes! The friar is without the gate, and he bears Cecily upon his horse. He begs admission!"

Their eyes met, wide with disbelief.

"Why has this rude friar come to our gate at so late an hour," the abbess asked, her brow furrowed, "and why bears he Cecily?"

"I know not, Mother," replied Agnes. "But we should admit him and learn the truth of it."

"Very well, Sister. Novice, bid him enter, and see to his horse."

Moments later, Friar Thomas entered, bearing the unconscious girl in his arms. Water dripped from her robes, and her head, crowned with a golden circlet entwined with mistletoe, lolled against his shoulder.

"Lay her on the worktable, Friar," Agnes instructed, moving quickly to examine the girl. "And tell us, I pray you, what this portends."

Friar Thomas, with care, placed Cecily upon the table. Agnes drew back her sodden cloak, revealing a white robe clinging to her chilled frame, the mistletoe tangled in her hair.

"She was to be the Samhain sacrifice," the friar said grimly. "*The Kindred* had prepared her for the blade. When you denied me leave to pursue my inquiries, I took measures of my own. I placed a hidden brother among their number and learned of the ritual performed by the one they call the Archdruid, who serves as their High Sacrificer."

Agnes's face darkened. Beside her, Mother Alice turned pale, both women silenced by the gravity of the friar's words.

"We waited until the rite had neared its final moment. Then we struck. My men fell upon them from all sides. Many we captured—but not all."

"And what then of their leader, Friar?" asked Mother Alice.

Thomas's face was grave. "He escaped into the woods, Mother. And we still know not who he truly is."

Agnes frowned. "Friar, how came you to aid us, when once you would have condemned us?"

"Sister, it took but little time, once I had seen *The Kindred* for what they were, to know that they—not you—were the ones I sought. Alas, we have not caught them all, nor do we yet know the identity of the Archdruid. But methinks we shall make better progress together than apart."

Mother Alice nodded. "If that be so, Friar, mayhap we shall be rid of this darkness all the sooner. Your offer is acceptable. Sister?"

"Indeed, Mother," said Agnes. "The friar is forceful, and his men may well aid us in erasing this scourge, and the dark figure who commands them."

Agnes returned to her patient. Cecily stirred, sighed, and slowly sat up, rubbing her eyes. As the drugged wine wore off, her voice grew clearer, though she remained drowsy.

"How fare you, child?"

"I remember little," Cecily whispered. "Only waking once, upon the friar's horse... and now—this. Where am I? What has befallen me?"

"You are at the abbey. You drank wine laced with deadly herbs, Cecily," Agnes said gently. "The potion clouded your mind and showed you illusions. You were meant to die upon *The Kindred's* altar as a blood sacrifice. What say you now to returning to the abbey, and the penance that awaits?"

"That I will never do, Sister," Cecily replied. "The burden is more than I can bear. I came here not of my own will, but that is how I shall leave. I shall return to my parents and beg their forgiveness for the pain I caused."

Mother Alice pondered her words but a moment, then gave a slow nod. "Child, I perceive that you speak truly. Our cloistered life is a comfort to some, but a hardship to many. You are welcome to visit us for prayers and a meal. We shall pray for your safe return to your family."

The friar looked upon Cecily with a kindness that bordered on paternal. "Mayhap you will ride with me again, child. I shall see you safely home."

Cecily smiled faintly. "I would like that, Friar. And this time, I shall be awake to remember it…and at peace, knowing you'll be there to protect me."

Mother Alice smiled. "The blessing of God go with you, my child."

Alexis – New Revelations

Morning came, and though the night's travail had left Agnes, Mother Alice, and Isabel weary to the bone, it was time for prayers and the morning meal to break their fast. Yet ere the bell had rung, Alexis entered Agnes's workroom, her expression somber.

"I have spoken with one of the novices," she began. "She told me that, ere she came to Godstow, she did witness a sacrifice much like that nearly wrought here. It made her sore afraid, and she fled to our abbey seeking solace and sanctuary. Now, the sisters murmur of these dark rites, and many are grievously distressed."

Sister Agnes frowned. "If that be so, Alexis, then we needs must act swiftly to calm their fears."

"Forsooth, I fear it shall not be easy," Alexis replied. "The rumours grow of their own accord and now seem to live a life apart from those who first whispered them."

"Then I shall entreat Mother to speak at prayers," Agnes said. "Perchance her words shall serve as a balm. We must quell these rumours. They bring unrest and danger in their wake."

BOOK THE THIRD
THE INQUIRY DEEPENS

In which Lady Harriet continues her research, this time in the 21st-century Bodleian Library in Oxford. She takes up the telling of our story and experiences a rare time shift phenomenon, transporting her back to 1299.

Chapter 14
The Unquiet Past

Wherein we see, through Lady Harriet's research, the haunting nature of Beatrix's letters and their unresolved implications. We learn of the true source of the modern-day Lady Harriet's title, her 14th-century ancestor, and begin to unravel the mysteries surrounding The Kindred.

Lady Harriet sighed as she looked at her watch. How could another day have passed with her making so little progress?

She had successfully traced her family's lineage across continental Europe and Great Britain, even as far as the tiny Isle of Man, where she became fascinated with Celtic traditions and the chance to uncover a connection to the Druids.

Over the last week, she'd been deep in the special collections section of Oxford University's Bodleian Library, focusing on the Oxfordshire area. She thought that she might find a connection between her FitzAlan line and a prominent 14th-century family of the same name.

The day passed uneventfully, however, leaving Harriet somewhat frustrated. Again, she sighed. The brick walls she faced were as impenetrable as some of those of the library itself. Indeed, she should be able to find the answers she sought in one of the world's oldest libraries and the second-largest one in Britain. But she did not. *No. Stop,* she thought. *Just stop. You need a break. You need to clear your head.*

Little did Harriet know that she was about to stumble upon not the answers she sought, but a tale of murder hundreds of years old.

Here, Lady Harriet takes up our tale.

Lady Harriet – A Change of Approach

As certain as I was that I'd find the answers, I also knew that sometimes you have to step back to gain a different perspective. However, I couldn't shake the nagging feeling that I was overlooking something crucial. I knew I had seen something along the way that I should have paid more attention to, but I couldn't figure out what it was.

I left the long, wooden table with the soft lighting of the traditional green reading lamps and carried the box back to the librarian's small office.

"Good afternoon, Mrs. Wood. Here is the box of documents I've been working through, but I won't be back for a few days. Thank you so much for everything you have done and all the help you have given me."

"Oh, Lady Harriet, please don't give up. And you don't need to be so formal. Please call me Mary. I feel as though we are longtime friends, and I really want to help you."

Mary Wood was easily more than twice my age and couldn't have looked more the part of a librarian if she were to play the role in a BBC period drama. She was quite distinguished in appearance, with her silver-grey hair pulled back in a classic chignon that revealed tiny pearl earrings. She wore a well-made navy wool cardigan over a crisp white cotton blouse and a comfortable plaid skirt. Her sturdy brogues were surprisingly quiet, her footsteps nearly silent on the historic floors.

"Why, thank you, um…. Mary. It does seem we've known each other far longer than a week. Might I ask a favor?"

I handed her my Reader's Card. "When you have a moment, would you please check to see if you can find anything else that might relate to the FitzAlan family? Perhaps there's something in one of your rare collections. I would even be happy to look through items related to families living near the FitzAlan estate. I came across the name de Aylesbridge on some of Bodleian's excellent old maps. Maybe I'll find something there."

"Of course, Lady Harriet. I would be delighted to see what I can find. Go on now and treat yourself to a nice cuppa. I'd suggest The Vaults & Garden Café, just next door. Be sure to try one of their scones with clotted cream and homemade jam. Then, perhaps, a nice walk in one of the parks or gardens along the River Cherwell. That should help you collect your thoughts and get you back on track. Then you'll have a fresh start whenever you are ready to return to your research."

"Brilliant idea. Thank you again, Mrs. Wood. Mary. I will do just that. Who knows—I might be back sooner than you think."

Lady Harriet – Rewarded

I returned to my flat in Clevedon for a few days, and it was exactly what I needed. I breathed in the salt-tinged breeze as I walked along Clevedon's pebbly shore, letting the rhythmic wash of waves from the Bristol Channel clear my mind. After weeks bent over dusty old manuscripts and documents in Oxford's Bodleian Library, my little coastal garden had become completely overgrown. I found deep satisfaction in the mindless work of weeding between the spring daffodils and checking on my emerging pea shoots. My plan for a change of scenery was doing exactly what I'd hoped.

As I pruned the climbing roses that threatened to engulf my garden gate, two thoughts struck me at once: that curious phrase in the marginalia of the 15th-century manuscript wasn't a copying error at all— it was a deliberate cipher, and more importantly, the supposed death date of John FitzAlan's second wife couldn't possibly be correct, not with the baptismal records of their children that I'd found in the parish archives.

I rushed inside to pack my valise, knowing Mrs. Wood would be thrilled to help me pursue this new lead. Within the hour, I was racing back to Oxford.

Mary Wood - A Box of Treasures

By early afternoon, the honey-colored stone walls of the Bodleian Library welcomed me back as I hurried through its corridors toward Mrs. Wood's office. She was at her desk, hunched in that way all lifelong librarians seem to be—a testament to years spent poring over catalogue drawers and research requests. Her reading glasses caught the afternoon light as she studied the papers before her with characteristic intensity.

"Mary! Mary!" I fought to keep my voice at a whisper, barely containing my excitement. "I'm back, and you were absolutely right —a break from research was exactly what I needed. Not only did I finally remember what had been nagging at my subconscious, but I've discovered another thread I need to follow. Were you able to find anything promising?"

"Lady Harriet, welcome back! I must say, you look much better. I had started to worry about you."

With a twinkle in her eye, Mary Wood retrieved the box I'd returned when I had left so precipitously. "I suspected that you might remember what had piqued your interest earlier, so I kept these documents close instead of returning them to the stacks. Once you find what you're looking for, it should help guide your next steps. But that's not all."

She leaned in, lowering her voice conspiratorially. "I spent considerable time in our older storage facilities, many of them underground, connected by a tunnel system. I knew that if there was anything to find, it would be somewhere on those original wooden shelves. And I was right."

I collected the boxes and hurried to a quiet corner of the reading room, my footsteps quickening with anticipation. My instincts told me I was finally on the right track.

Settling at my research carrel worktable, I eyed both boxes before me. Common sense told me I should return to the original collection and pursue those questionable FitzAlan baptismal records, but the new box beckoned irresistibly. My fingers were already reaching for the lid of Mary's box when I caught myself. "For heaven's sake, Harriet, focus!" I murmured, pulling on the cotton gloves I'd nearly forgotten in my excitement.

Inside, layers of archival tissue cradled the contents like delicate snowdrifts. As I peeled back the protective sheets, a treasure trove emerged: documents dating back seven centuries, timeworn parchments, vellum scrolls, and hand-bound books. Among them, I spotted what looked like personal correspondence and perhaps even a diary, each bearing the careful preservation marks of generations of archivists. Within these protective layers, clues in a long-buried story or a forgotten document might be waiting to surface.

And they were.

Lady Harriet – Enigmatic Correspondence

The label on the box immediately drew my eye: *"de Aylesbridge Collection: Late 13th to Early 14th Century"*. My heart quickened —the de Aylesbridges had once held lands adjacent to the FitzAlan estate. Perhaps this unexpected detour would lead me exactly where I needed to go.

Well, a quick look won't hurt, I thought to myself, my practiced hands moving with the reverence of a curator across the aged documents. I breathed in the musty scent of ancient parchment as I methodically sorted through the contents.

Through my study of early maps and land conveyance records, I discovered a geographic connection between the FitzAlans and the de Aylesbridges. Entries in some of the earliest forms of census records, the Domesday Book and The Hundred Rolls, confirmed it. When my eyes caught the words "Lady Beatrix," my breath caught. The name sparked an instant connection across the centuries to my own dear friend, Bea, also a Lady, though with the more modern spelling, Lady Beatrice. It was as if history itself were winking at me.

With the utmost care, I lifted a parchment from the top of what appeared to be a collection of business documents of some sort. Faint in the corner, the de Aylesbridge family crest remained where a wax seal once secured the parchment against prying eyes. Slowly and with great care, I examined it. It was the first of several documents that I discovered mentioning Lady Beatrix. More than an hour slipped by before I reached the final piece: a detailed record of her family's generous gifts and endowments to Godstow Abbey.

Where to look next, I wondered, as another item in the box caught my eye. Nestled at the bottom was a small bundle of letters, tied neatly with a faded silk ribbon, once a defiant scarlet. Even in medieval times, it seemed people cherished their personal correspondence enough to keep it, just as I did.

As I gently loosened the delicate knot, the differences between the letters became apparent. Even before I read a word, each piece of vellum told its own story. Multiple hands had penned these messages, and the distinct styles ranged from loops and flourishes to sharp, angular strokes and imprecise rounded letters. The topmost letter crackled softly as I unfolded it. I leaned forward, using a magnifying glass to examine the vellum, eager to begin deciphering the text and unlocking its secrets. For now, my focus was on Beatrix.

These letters had me spellbound. The carefully preserved pages seemed to pulse with untold stories, more compelling than any other breakthrough I could hope for. As I smoothed each page, patterns began to emerge—the anxious slant of the writing, the heavy-handed quill strokes, the hurriedly sealed edges.

What I had read so far hinted at something darker, something unsettling that had upended Beatrix's life. The words between the lines spoke louder than the text itself—veiled references that set my historian's instincts tingling. I caught glimpses of a romance gone awry, suspicions lurking, and a danger that loomed just out of reach. I had to know what had happened to this medieval woman whose story had lain silent for centuries, waiting for someone to finally piece it together.

The letters appeared to come from two different correspondents over the course of several weeks, followed by a third, smaller group. These, only partially written, were unfinished and unsent. One began: "My Noble Lord," but continued no further. Several others started in a similar manner, continuing for just a few lines, often with words crossed out, before abruptly stopping. The ink had faded badly, leaving only scattered phrases and words visible:

> *"To the Most Honorable Lord Edwin, my heart*
> *rebels against the thought that you have not..."*

"My Noble Lord, that which I must convey weighs heavily upon my spirit. Your words of devotion…"

"To Lord Edwin de Ravenswold, I pray this finds you well. Recent revelations have caused me to…"

"I cannot reconcile what I now know with…"

"Truth" was legible in the margin, the rest scratched out.

"My Noble Lord, the weight of silence has become unbearable."

The following line bore deep, angry slashes that cut through the words, followed by a large ink blot, as if her hand had trembled and spilled the ink.

The handwriting was elegant and precise, its flowing letters more restrained than I'd seen in some of the others. *These must be letters that Lady Beatrix started and never finished*, I thought. But why? They hinted at inner turmoil and suggested a difficult period in her life, which compelled her to attempt, again and again, to write to Edwin de Ravenswold, only to falter each time.

Intrigued and captivated by what I'd found, yet thoroughly puzzled, I leaned back in my chair to think about how to proceed. These were more than simple historical curiosities. They were fragments of a deeper mystery that I wanted to solve. I glanced around the quiet reading room of the Bodleian and felt a tangible connection to the centuries-old voices speaking to me through these pages.

Lady Harriet, The Professor –
Echoes of a Far Distant Past

The scent of aged leather and parchment enveloped me as I rummaged through the box of documents, searching for a connection that would transport me to the past. Would it help me unravel the mysteries I was certain lay hidden in 13th and 14th-century Oxfordshire?

My fingers trembled—not from the autumn chill seeping through the library's stone walls, but from sheer anticipation as I sifted through the box. Each document was a potential key to unlocking those mysteries.

I froze. Beneath a stack of ordinary documents lay a thick parchment, its surface still bearing the unmistakable seal of Balliol College, Oxford. Though dulled by centuries, the wax retained its sharp impression. The letter's script flowed confidently across the page, the iron gall ink still bold and unfaded. At the bottom, the signature was one I did not recognize— "Professor Reginald Barrington."

"Who was this professor?" I wondered. Forcing myself to follow proper procedure, I donned fresh cotton gloves and gently unfolded the vellum, careful not to crack or damage its delicate surface. Then I began to read. The salutation stopped me in my tracks: "To Lady Harriet FitzAlan."

My name. My title. How could that be? It was impossible.

The title "Lady", long dismissed as nothing more than quaint family lore, wrapped in vague tales of a brother lost to the Crusades, was something tangible—something real. With reluctant discipline, I set aside the professor's letter and turned to the college archives. Professor Barrington, I discovered, was far more than just another Oxford don – he was a graduate of Balliol College and a renowned medievalist whose travels had taken him from the scriptoriums of Mont Saint-Michel to the dusty archives of Constantinople.

I returned to the box in search of clues, and, within minutes, uncovered a Letters Patent, its formal language cutting through the centuries:

> In the 35th year of Henry, by the grace of God, King of England, Duke of Aquitaine, and Lord of Ireland, upon the Feast of St. Michael, the title of Lady was conferred upon Harriet FitzAlan in recognition of her family's noble service and the sacrifice of her brother in the holy cause.

I stopped, stunned. The weight of history pressed against me. Here was proof—my title was no mere affectation, but a memorial carved in a brother's blood and sacrifice. More importantly, it hinted at the connection I'd begun to suspect between the FitzAlans and the de Aylesbridge family. The contents of the box were beginning to make sense.

I turned back to Professor Barrington's letter addressed to my long-lost ancestor. In his precise script unfolded a tale of intrigue centered on Lady Beatrix, whose actions had nearly destroyed both families and shaken the very foundations of Godstow Abbey itself. Sister Agnes, Beatrix's confidante and close friend within the Abbey's walls, emerged as a pivotal figure in a drama that still echoed through time.

I slowly removed my reading glasses, setting them gently beside the scattered documents on the worktable. The tears that had gathered in my eyes as I read further threatened to fall as I returned to the librarian's office. Mary looked up from her desk, concern flickering across her weathered face.

"Child," she said, rising from her chair, "what's troubling you? You look as though you've seen a ghost."

"I have, Mary. A nine-hundred-year-old ghost living in the selfsame box you brought me."

Mary guided me to a chair, her lined face soft with understanding. "Here, sit. Have some tea." She poured from the ever-present pot on her desk, the scent of steeping leaves filling the small office. "Now then, tell me everything. What secrets has our little library unearthed that have shaken you so?"

I wrapped my hands around the warm cup, willing my thoughts into order. How could I explain that inside that box lay not just documents but bridges across time? Through everything I had uncovered, I could almost hear Beatrix's voice, whispering secrets from the past.

Lady Harriet – Back Home

After nearly a week spent poring over the letters and documents from the box, deciphering their spidery script, and adding my own careful annotations, my body demanded respite. I glanced at my watch. Half four. I was tired. Bone, dog tired. My eyes burned, my back ached, and exhaustion had settled deep in my bones. My mind refused to process another word of medieval intrigue, let alone make sense of it all. It was time to return these precious boxes to Mary and finally head home.

Mary rose to meet me as I stopped by her office to say goodbye. "You've been an extraordinary help, Mary, but more than that, a dear friend. But now, I need to go home and make sense of everything I have learned. There is a story here, Mary, and it's not a pleasant one."

"You'll manage splendidly, Lady Harriet," she assured me, her eyes twinkling. "You are made of stern stuff. I see unwavering resolve and determination in you. You must come back and share what you discover."

"Thank you, Mary. But for now, I should start the journey home. It is nearly 95 miles to Clevedon, and I want to be there by supper."

By the time I arrived, all I wanted was a cup of hot cocoa, a few biscuits, and a good night's sleep in my own bed. I pulled into my building's car park, gathered my belongings, and locked my classic Morris Minor. I hauled my valise and briefcase, bulging with notes and transcriptions, up two flights of stairs to my flat. At my door, I paused, key in hand, and smiled. Home.

My flat wasn't luxurious, but it was spacious, with magnificent views of the broad Severn Estuary on one side and Clevedon's rolling hills on the other. As a corner unit, my flat boasted abundant large windows—a later addition to the original Victorian architecture. I loved nothing more than settling into my favorite fireside chair, watching the sunset paint Clevedon Pier an ever-changing palette of color, tea in hand— or, occasionally, something a little stronger.

The building's venerable age gave it a comforting, homey feel, and I did not mind living there alone. Widowed long ago, I felt no need for male companionship. As my mum once said, I was content in my own company. Besides, I had my research. I had a passion for gathering the loose threads from my historical charts and working with them until they could be woven into the fabric of family histories.

But tonight, I simply was tired. I heated milk for my cocoa and arranged a few biscuits on a plate. I tossed a fresh scoop of coal into the old Victorian stove—a nod to the past but also a practical necessity—then slipped into my comfiest nightgown to settle in for the evening. As I changed, my grandmother's brooch caught my eye from its spot on my dressing table—an annular piece of silver adorned with garnets, passed down through generations of FitzAlan women. I touched it briefly, recalling how Gran had presented it on my eighteenth birthday with great ceremony. "It's medieval," she told me, "and it has quite a history, though most of it has been lost to time."

"Cocoa, biscuits, and bed," I murmured sleepily. "Perfect." After the week's revelations, my antique four-poster, thick goose-down duvet, and feather pillows beckoned like a lover's arms.

As I tucked into my evening treat, I wondered where the documents and letters from the library might lead. The idea of being a "fly on the wall" as these intrigues unfolded utterly fascinated me. How, for instance, were the people in the letters connected? Why the particular focus on Lady Beatrix? Was my ancestor somehow entangled in this curious web?

My thoughts began to unravel, slipping from question to question, until weariness dulled the edges of my curiosity.

Cup empty and plate bare, I was asleep almost before my head touched the pillows.

Then the dream came.

Chapter 15
To Sleep, Perchance to Dream

In which we see the events described in the documents discovered by Lady Harriet in the library's collection through her eyes.

As Harriet drifted off to sleep, the transition unfolded subtly yet profoundly—almost at once, she began to dream. It didn't take long for her to sense something had changed. The shadows of her cozy flat solidified into stone walls, and the weight of her comfortable nightgown and the duvet shifted into the elaborate folds of a noblewoman's gown. She had stepped out of her world into that of Lady Harriet and Lady Beatrix. She recognized this phenomenon from her research—the rare temporal shift experienced by only the most lucid dreamers. No theory could prepare her for the visceral reality of standing in a medieval great hall. Yet here she was.

The hall itself seemed to breathe history—tapestries of hunting scenes adorned the walls, while sconces cast a warm glow across the stone floor. Draped in the grand gown and cloak of a high-born Lady, she stood in the very manor house granted to her late brother by King Henry himself, and, with his death, she was now of the nobility. Lady Harriet was one of the rare high-born ladies who had inherited their titles in their own right. With the title came responsibility—villages, farms, and countless lives depended upon her judgment.

Her hand moved unconsciously to her throat, where the silver brooch, the same one that had been on her dressing table moments ago, now fastened her heavy velvet cloak. The familiar weight of it helped anchor her between the two realities she straddled.

A young page approached, his steps echoing in the vast space. His slight frame shrank further as he bowed deeply before her, eyes fixed firmly on the floor. "My Lady," he began, voice barely above a whisper, "a scholar stands without, seeking audience. He speaks of a matter most urgent and humbly entreats your swift attention."

Drawing upon what felt like borrowed memories, Lady Harriet spoke with more confidence than she felt. "Bid him enter, good page. We shall hear what business brings a man of learning to our hall at this hour."

The figure who entered was familiar to her—both to her waking self and to the one who moved within the dream. It was Professor Barrington, his academic robes billowing as he strode forward. "My Lady," he said, his voice tight with urgency, "you must accompany me to the abbey without delay. Sister Agnes awaits us on a matter of grave importance. My carriage stands ready."

As she navigated carefully in her unfamiliar attire on their way to the abbey, Harriet's mind worked on two levels. Her dream-self knew Sister Agnes as a trusted friend and confidante, while her modern consciousness recalled the description of the Benedictine nun from Professor Barrington's letter: "The Abbey's infirmarist, supervisor of the infirmary, accomplished healer, herbalist, nurse and anatomist—and, of late, investigator of murders."

The abbey's infirmary, when they reached it, was a study in contrasts. Neat rows of herbs hung drying from the ceiling, their pungent scents mixing with the sweeter aroma of healing unguents. Sister Agnes stood at her worktable, grinding herbs with focused precision, but her hands stilled as they entered. Even in the dream,

Harriet could sense the tension in the air. Something was terribly wrong at Godstow Abbey, and she had a feeling both versions of herself would uncover the truth.

The professor spoke with conviction. "Sister, you must dissuade your friend, Lady Beatrix, from making so grave an error in judgment. Such a choice could bring ruin upon her house and endanger the abbey itself."

Sister Agnes looked up from the herbs she was grinding methodically with her mortar and pestle, her eyes reflecting concern as she fixed her gaze upon the professor.

"Of what peril do you speak? Perchance it is Lord Edwin's interest in Lady Beatrix that you mean?" She lowered her voice but spoke with steady resolve. "I, too, have noted that his presence in her life coincides with her growing hesitation to aid us in our investigations."

The professor stepped close, his voice low and deliberate.

"There are whispers most troubling, Sister. People say that they saw him in the woods beyond the abbey grounds, partaking in gatherings that bear more likeness to heathen rites than to Christian prayer. I do fear his intent toward Lady Beatrix is false, and that he seeks not her heart, but to turn her away from uncovering truths that might imperil his…cohorts."

Harriet watched the scene unfold, feeling strangely present yet distant, as one does in dreams. She took in the infirmary's stone walls, which held both warmth and shadow, as the professor spoke. Something about Lord Edwin's name stirred a memory she could not fully grasp, as if she'd encountered it before—or would in another time.

Sister Agnes set down her mortar.

"Lady Beatrix has ever shown good wisdom in matters of both heart and duty. Yet since first she met Lord Edwin at the Michaelmas feast, she speaks of little else but his poetry, learning, and noble bearing. When I do name Thomas of Hereford's murder or the sacrificed young swine and mysterious monkshood discovered in the abbey's garden, she grows distant and turns the discourse elsewhere."

"This is precisely what troubles me," the professor pressed. "Each time we draw nigh to some revelation of these dark matters, Lord Edwin turns her thoughts elsewhere—be it a romantic ride, a gift of rare spices, or some new tale of his travels. Such cannot be mere happenstance."

Through the dream haze, Harriet experienced a distinct duality of perspective, as though she were both an observer and a participant. The name "Harriet" resonated, not as her own, but as belonging to another Harriet who had walked these same corridors centuries prior and had also harboured suspicions about Lord Edwin.

She touched the brooch at her throat with a sense of faith, believing it would guide and protect her. The reassuring presence of the brooch, imbued with personal meaning and ancestral connection, began to return her to her flat in Clevedon.

As the dream faded, Harriet again was aware of her familiar surroundings and the bright sunshine pouring through her windows. Stretching and pulling her robe tighter about her, she arose and went to the old stove, adding coal and building up the fire against the early morning chill.

As she put a pot on to brew her morning tea, she wondered, "Whatever happened? It was as if I was back in time, watching a story unfold before my eyes—the same story teased by the parchments and vellums at the library. I must return and follow up on these hints. For now, though, tea and a sticky bun or two will help get me going."

With that, she poured her tea, put the buns on a delicate china plate, and settled down before her window, enjoying her breakfast and watching the waters below.

Lady Harriet had no idea where those hints would take her research. Was there danger here?

Chapter 16
Whispers of Deceit

In which friends warn Lady Beatrix of treachery entering her life.

Lady Beatrix de Aylesbridge approached the weathered gates of Godstow Abbey, her heart tangled with curiosity and uncertainty. The message had been brief, near cryptic—a missive from Sister Agnes, the infirmarist and a dear friend, bidding her to come without delay.

As the coachman assisted her down from the carriage, Beatrix gathered the folds of her dark green woolen cloak, embroidered at the hem with her family's crest. She glanced up at the abbey's imposing façade, where arched windows reflected the waning light of day. The cool air bore the faint scents of lavender and rosemary, mingling with the damp, earthen fragrance of aged stone. Beatrix stepped onto the narrow path leading to the main entrance, the toll of a distant bell echoing softly through the cloistered grounds.

A young novice, her plain woolen habit hanging loose upon her slight frame, opened the door and dipped into a swift curtsy. The habit's coarse grey fabric marked her as one not yet fully vowed, and the simple knotted cord at her waist bore none of the tokens of a professed nun. "This way, My Lady," the girl murmured, her voice barely above a whisper. She turned and led Beatrix along the well-trodden corridors toward the infirmary.

Sister Agnes was not one to summon without cause. Their friendship spanned many years, yet seldom had the infirmarist called upon her with such urgency. Beatrix's thoughts turned to dark possibilities—illness, perhaps, or some hidden trouble festering within the abbey's walls.

By the time they reached Sister Agnes's workroom, Beatrix's apprehension had settled into a persistent knot in her chest. The novice rapped softly, her small hand barely making a sound against the ancient wood, and she eased the door open. Inside, the room was warm and fragrant with the scents of dried herbs and beeswax candles, their flickering light casting shadows across the shelves lined with jars and pots.

Sister Agnes – Lady Beatrix

Beatrix took a steadying breath and stepped inside, masking her unease behind a warm smile. Whatever news awaited her here, she would face it with the same strength and grace she had cultivated through years of courtly life.

Sister Agnes felt a heaviness in her spirit as she saw Beatrix's smile. Though she understood the professor's counsel, she faltered at the weight of this delicate task. How was she to warn her dear friend without wounding her heart? After embracing Beatrix in greeting, she drew back, filled with a quiet sadness. Gathering her courage, she lowered her voice and murmured,

"My Lady, I pray you, take heed of this new courtship. I fear it may bring you to ruin. I have made supplication unto the Blessed Virgin, and by her counsel, I must speak plain. This path could well lead to sorrow. Mayhap, he is not what he seems."

Lady Beatrix lifted her gaze, surprise flickering in her eyes.

"Sister Agnes, you speak so severely. What brings you to such a conclusion about Lord Edwin? He has shown only kindness and generosity unto me."

Sister Agnes folded her hands tightly before her and drew a deep breath as she sought the right words.

"It is his very kindness that troubles me, My Lady. At the Michaelmas feast, he laboured much to place himself at your side, speaking with such ease and grace. Yet his words carried the shadow of deceit. I fear he fashioned his deeds to turn you from your purpose."

"What purpose do you mean, Sister? He shares his love of poetry, brings me thoughtful gifts, and even offers his aid in our investigations at the abbey."

As she spoke, confusion and a pang of sadness stirred within her. How could those closest to her doubt the sincerity of Edwin's attentions, or her own judgment?

Sister Agnes inclined her head, her voice gentle but firm.

"Ah, My Lady, therein lies my concern. His gifts and fair speech may blind you to his true intent. His offers of aid seem not to further our cause, but to draw you from our true path, to hinder rather than to help. His behavior persuades me that he would turn your eyes from the matter we pursue with the novice Isabel. Greater things hang in the balance than courtship alone."

Beatrix sighed.

"Lady Harriet, my dearest friend, has questioned me about Lord Edwin's intent, though not so directly as do you, Sister Agnes. Yet I am no longer in the bloom of youth. The years slip by, and I fear growing old in solitude. What if his heart is true? When he speaks, there is earnestness in his words, a warmth that stirs my heart. Could it be that his love is honest, and I wrong him by doubting his character without just cause?"

"Dearest Beatrix, the bonds of matrimony are not a measure of your worth. You possess intelligence, generosity, kindness, and steadfastness of spirit. Lord Edwin's ways may be enticing, yet we must look beyond appearances. Pray, consider that his motives may not be pure. It is better to be cautious than to bestow trust unwisely and invite sorrow."

Sister Agnes reached out to hold her hand as Beatrix lowered her gaze, thoughts clouded.

"Your words give me pause, Sister Agnes, yet I am torn. How shall I discern the truth of his intentions?"

Sister Agnes offered a comforting smile, her voice soft.

"Pray for wisdom, My Lady. Watch his deeds, for they shall reveal his heart more truly than his words. Seek the counsel of trusted friends, such as Lady Harriet. Trust in the Blessed Virgin to guide you and illuminate the truth. If Lord Edwin's love be true, it shall endure both scrutiny and time. If it is not, better the pain of knowing now than a sorrow that lingers."

Beatrix nodded slowly, a measure of resolve settling upon her.

"You are wise, Sister Agnes. I shall take your counsel to heart and tread with care. Your words and the guidance of the Blessed Virgin shall lead me."

Sister Agnes gently squeezed Beatrix's hand, her gaze warm with reassurance.

"Be at ease, My Lady. You do not face this alone. Together, we shall uncover the truth."

In the quiet of that moment, the bond between the two women deepened, trust and friendship weaving their hearts together. Beatrix felt a spark of hope and determination take root within her. Whatever mask Lord Edwin might wear, she would see through it—for the sake of her friends, her faith, and her own peace.

Lady Beatrix – A Letter from Cousin Eleanor

The crisp autumn air carried the scent of damp leaves and woodsmoke as a lone page rode up to the gates of Aylesbridge Manor. Clad in the crimson and silver of the Hawthorne Estate, the lad, who looked no older than fourteen, dismounted swiftly. He handed the reins to a stable hand and presented a wax-sealed scroll to the porter.

The porter, a stout man bundled against the chill, squinted at the boy before stepping forward.

"From Hawthorne, are ye?" he asked gruffly.

"Aye, sir," the page replied, his voice steady but boyish. "I bear a letter for Lady Beatrix de Aylesbridge."

The porter nodded and inspected the red wax seal, its imprint bearing the emblem of Hawthorne—a cluster of serrated hawthorn leaves and berries. Satisfied, he handed the letter to the waiting steward. The steward accepted the letter with a curt nod, his face betraying no curiosity.

"Wait here," he instructed the page before turning and vanishing down the corridor.

Seated in her chambers at her writing table, the golden light of autumn streaming in caught the rich chestnut of Beatrix's elegantly braided hair. The knock at the door drew her attention, and she called out, "Enter."

The steward stepped inside, bowing slightly as he presented the wax-sealed scroll upon a silver tray. "A letter, My Lady, from Hawthorne."

Beatrix's lips curved into a smile as she reached for the scroll. "From Eleanor?" she asked, her voice lifting with anticipation.

"I believe so, My Lady."

With a gracious nod, Beatrix dismissed the steward, her fingers already moving to break the seal. As she read Eleanor's missive, her smile faltered, a faint crease marring her brow. When she reached the bottom of the page, her hands tightened upon the letter, and she murmured,

"Eleanor cannot be speaking the truth…yet why does my heart feel troubled?"

A shadow of worry passed over her face as she drew a slow breath, willing herself to be calm. With a soft sigh, she rose from her writing table, picked up the parchment, and crossed the chamber to the carved chest where her shawl lay neatly folded on top. She wrapped the woolen garment snugly about her shoulders and made her way down the stone staircase.

Beyond the heavy doors at the rear of the manor, the gardens stretched before her, still and resplendent in their autumn hues. The morning frost clung to the grass, glimmering like tiny jewels in the sunlight.

Beatrix walked with measured steps to her favorite spot—a weathered stone bench beneath the sprawling branches of a great oak. There, she sank onto the cold stone, drawing her shawl tightly around her. Her fingers traced the familiar wax seal; her thoughts drifted to Eleanor.

Her cousin. One of her dearest friends. Her memories were vivid as if no time had passed—summers spent chasing Eleanor through the vast gardens of Hawthorne Hall, their laughter ringing like birdsong in the warm air. Their family lands lay divided by a winding stream, where they had waded barefoot, lifting their skirts to catch darting minnows.

As they grew, their activities softened into quieter pursuits—whispering confidences by firelight, murmuring about which squires caught their eye at festival dances, and weaving elaborate stories about the noble knights and stately ladies whose portraits lined the halls of their manors.

The same stern-faced tutor instructed them in letters and Latin, as well as in household management and scripture. Eleanor had always followed Beatrix, eager to learn, her wide blue eyes filled with admiration and love. Beatrix had guided her through it all—from her first faltering steps in a courtly dance to the quiet heartbreak of a suitor's rejection. They had been as close as sisters, their bond unshaken by the years that had passed.

And now Eleanor's letter lay in her hands, its tone unlike the cheerful missives she so often sent. Beatrix's chest tightened as she unrolled it once more, the words pulling her back to the present. A cool breeze stirred loose strands of her hair as she read, her expression shifting between concern and contemplation.

Seeking solace in the pale warmth of the sun, Beatrix let out a slow breath and smoothed the parchment. In the quiet beauty of the garden, she began again, reading Eleanor's words slowly, from the very beginning.

> Dearest and Most Beloved Cousin Beatrix,
>
> I pray this letter finds you in good health and blessed spirits, for nothing brings me greater comfort than the knowledge that you are well. Yet my heart is heavy as I take quill to parchment. I beseech you to read on, knowing that these words come from the depths of my love and steadfast devotion.

This concerns Lord Edwin de Ravenswold. It grieves me deeply to cast a shadow upon what should be a time of joy, yet I cannot remain silent.

At the first, his attentions to you at Michaelmas gladdened me also. His discourse upon the art of illuminating manuscripts and his knowledge of healing herbs bespoke a man of learning and refinement, and I found him most agreeable in manner. Yet, since the feast, I have been much unsettled, and I feel it is my duty to share with you something I did witness.

While the hall was yet abounding with revelry, I beheld Lord Edwin in the company of one whose name I dare not write, though he is known to both of us. Their speech was low, and though I caught but fragments, I heard mention of "the circle" and "a gathering after the frost." The manner of it disturbs me.

Even more troubling, on the second day following Michaelmas, as I walked near the market with my father, Lord Edwin conversed with a man, a traveler, by his garb. They spoke in hushed tones, and I caught mention of gatherings held by moonlight and symbols drawn in sacred places. Their words sent a chill through me that I cannot shake.

Nor was this the last cause for my disquiet. Upon the most recent market day, I observed Lord Edwin in close discourse with the merchant woman, Magdalena, who, whispers say, deals in wares far beyond foreign spices. They exchanged small parcels with such furtiveness that it stirred my suspicions anew.

I write these things with a trembling hand, for I know how your heart has opened unto him. Yet I would sooner risk your momentary displeasure than hold my peace and thus fail you, should my fears prove true. You have been my guiding star and my wisest counsel, even from our earliest days. If I have erred in judgment, I shall humbly beseech your forgiveness —and his.

I pray you, forgive me if I have spoken amiss or caused you any sorrow, for such was never my intent. If my fears are unfounded, I shall count it a mercy and never speak of this matter again.

You are ever in my prayers, dearest Beatrix, as you have always been in my heart. May God guide and protect you in all things.

Your most loving and faithful cousin,

Eleanor of Hawthorne

Chapter 17
Courting in the Shadows

Wherein we learn of Edwin's courtship of Lady Beatrix, yet a shadow may veil its true purpose.

Beatrix drew her fur-lined mantle more tightly about her, hastening her steps against the chill of the autumn night. The air was crisp, her breath rising in pale wisps, then vanishing into the darkness. Overhead, the heavens lay strewn with a thousand stars, their cold fire indifferent to the tumult in her breast. She took no heed of their beauty, her thoughts fixed upon a single purpose.

A third warning, now. First from Sister Agnes, then from her dear friend, Lady Harriet, and now from Eleanor. All spoke of Lord Edwin—her Edwin—his intentions cast in shadow. Could it be true? Could he be false? She must know.

Edwin – Ravenswold

The de Ravenswold family had held their lands for centuries, their claim stretching back to a time when England warred against an enemy long since faded from memory. The oldest of local legends spoke of that battle—a day when a king's knight, grievously wounded, had fallen to the blood-soaked earth.

As the enemy pressed forward, a great black raven descended from the sky, alighting upon the knight's shoulder. Whether it whispered to him or merely served as an omen, none could say. But the knight rose, wounds forgotten, and the tide of battle turned. Victory won, in gratitude the king granted the knight vast swaths of land, dense and wild with ancient oaks, to hold in perpetuity. The knight named his holding Ravenswold—Raven's Wood—and in recognition of his valor, the king raised him to the nobility, bestowing upon him the title Lord of Ravenswold. His descendants have bound their bloodline to it, and the title endures.

Yet even before the family's rise, the land had held its own secrets. The estate of Ravenswold stood upon a natural rise, northwest of Oxford, where three towering oak trees still stood in an almost unnatural triangular formation. The Druids had favored such alignments for their sacred spaces. The oldest oak, gnarled and hollow at its core, was once rumored to have cradled the golden sickle of a powerful archdruid—a relic lost to time.

And beneath the estate? Passages.

The cellars ran unusually deep, so deep that even the servants spoke in hushed tones of corridors leading to underground chambers. Some called them mere storage vaults, yet others swore they led to ceremonial caves—places of power. Lord Edwin de Ravenswold had forbidden entry to the lowest levels, citing concerns over their stability.

Yet on certain nights, particularly during the old Celtic festivals, strange chants echoed up through the ventilation shafts.

None dared ask Lord Edwin about them.

Some things were best left undisturbed.

Lady Beatrix - Edwin

The path wound its way toward a gazebo, its timbers pale beneath the moon's silver light. There he stood, waiting. Clad in sable, his cloak bore the de Ravenswold crest—three silver ravens perched upon a blackened oak. The embroidery shimmered faintly in the dim glow, as though the birds might take wing. It was an old emblem, older than the name itself, some whispered. To most, it spoke of faith—the Trinity, the righteous emerging from darkness into light. Yet there were those who murmured of other meanings, far older ones.

Edwin stood tall, unmoving, his gaze fixed upon her. He was ever a striking figure—handsome, broad of chest, his bearing that of a man who bent not to the will of others. And now, he made no step forward, no gesture of greeting, as though he had known she would come to him.

Her heart pounded against her ribs, caught between hope and fear.

Beatrix quickened her pace, her breath coming fast, though whether from the chill night air or the sight of him, she could not say. Edwin's arms opened, and she went to him willingly, pressing into his embrace. His warmth enveloped her, the strength of him unmistakable.

Their lips met, the kiss deepening as longing overtook caution. His hands, firm yet reverent, traced the curve of her back, drawing her closer. The scent of him—leather, embers, and something darker, more elusive—sent a shiver down her spine as he reached up, quietly loosening the ties of her coif and veil. The fine linen slipped free, and her chestnut hair tumbled over her shoulders like unbound silk.

Edwin's fingers wove through the loose strands, a low murmur escaping his lips as he pressed another kiss to her mouth, then lower, the heat of his breath against her cheek and neck.

"God's mercy, Beatrix," he whispered, "do you know what it does to me, seeing you thus?"

His voice, thick with desire, sent heat coursing through her veins. She knew she should pull away, should speak of the warnings, the doubts that had plagued her. But here, in his arms, the world beyond seemed distant, inconsequential.

"My dearest Beatrix," he murmured, his voice like velvet, "since last we met in the orchard, I have thought of naught but you. All I beheld was your face, and the world was only you and me beneath the moon. I swore to you then, as I do now, that my heart is yours alone."

He gently tilted her face toward him, his gaze deep and searching.

"Did you not say that you could trust me with your soul? That in my arms, all else faded away? That I was your safe harbour, your solace?" A shadow of a smile touched his lips. "I remember how your laughter danced upon the wind, like a song meant for me alone. How your fingers clung to mine, as though the world beyond did not exist."

He lingered at her temple, lips warm against her skin, his voice dipping into something softer, more insistent.

"Yet now, you summon me here, in the hush of night, and I hear doubt in your voice. Tell me, sweet Beatrix, what fears have others placed in your heart?"

His hands tightened ever so slightly at her waist.

"I know of the words whispered to you, the warnings, the foolish talk meant to drive a wedge between us. What be their purpose but to part us? Would you let them steal what we have?"

His lips brushed against her brow.

"These whispers, these fearful mutterings of those in the abbey and wary kin—what be they but the ramblings and conjurings of the fearful? They see demons lurking in the dark where only shadows dwell. But I tell you, sweet Beatrix, there be no devils, no wicked spirits."

A shudder passed through Beatrix, not of passion, but of something colder, something she could not name. The warmth of Edwin's embrace should have reassured her, yet his words... his words unsettled her. It was not their meaning that gave her pause, but the way they fell from his lips.

The wind stirred the trees, rustling the last of the autumn leaves, and Beatrix suddenly felt as though the night itself were listening.

Her heart pounded, but not from longing. Something within her —something beyond reason, beyond sense—urged her to pull away.

She shifted against him, pressing her hands to his chest.

"Edwin..." she began, but the word faltered as she tried to step back.

His arms did not tighten to hold her, yet for a moment, it was as though she could not move.

Her breath caught.

The gazebo stood silent around her, the ivy along its pillars shifting in the wind. Beyond its open archways, the garden stretched into deep shadows beneath the night sky. She forced herself to step back, the heavy folds of her skirts brushing over the wooden floor.

The space where Edwin had stood moments before was empty. The warmth of his body had vanished, replaced by the cold of the autumn night, seeping into her skin.

She looked up.

Edwin was gone.

The night yawned open before her, vast and silent. Somewhere in the distance, an owl called—a lonely, haunting sound.

Her breath came fast, her pulse hammering against her throat. Slowly, she turned in a circle.

No retreating footsteps. No sign of movement through the gardens.

Only the bouquet of Michaelmas asters, fallen at her feet.

Edwin – the Sect

After his encounter with Lady Beatrix, Edwin returned to the stone circle hidden deep within the woods of his estate. He strode with purpose toward the great stone altar, where the Archdruid stood in solemn vigil. The scent of damp earth and the whisper of unseen wings wove through the sacred grove. High above, a raven perched upon the gnarled bough of an ancient oak, its black eyes gleaming like shards of obsidian in the moonlight.

"What news do you bring, Edwin de Ravenswold?" the Archdruid demanded, his voice cutting through the stillness of the night. "Has the lady agreed to cease her meddling in our affairs? Speak!"

"She is uncertain, oh Master of the Mists and Keeper of the Sacred Flame," Edwin replied, lowering his head in deference. "The meddling nun, and now her cousin, a mere slip of a girl, seek to turn her from me. Yet I believe I have sown enough doubt to keep her from prying further. Time shall tell."

"We have no time, you witless dullard!" the Archdruid thundered, his gaze sharp and unrelenting. "If we cannot still her fears, we must offer her as a sacrifice to the gods. Such is the will of the Old Ways."

Edwin hesitated, but only for a breath. Then, with steady conviction, he bowed his head and spoke.

"As you command, Lord Harbinger of the Old Gods. As you decree, so shall it be."

A gust of wind stirred the branches above, sending brittle oak leaves cascading around them. The raven let out a sharp, knowing caw, a sound both dark and ominous.

The Archdruid studied Edwin in silence before speaking again.

"And what of the girl? You claimed to love her once, did you not? Can you deceive her so easily?"

Edwin's lips twisted into a cruel smirk.

"Love?" he scoffed. "She is useful—nothing more. I have given her reason to believe my affections are true, but she is wary. She suspects. I must move swiftly to draw her close again, to rekindle her trust. Only then will her doubts be fully dispelled."

Unconvinced, the Archdruid spoke.

"See to it. If she cannot be swayed, her fate is already written. The gods are hungry—and they will not be denied."

Chapter 18
Confronting The Kindred

In which the investigation leads to confrontations with novices and individuals outside the abbey, pointing toward an organized plot.

Winter was coming on. Icy blasts of air made the abbey cold and drafty. The sisters all wore their heaviest habits and stayed close to the nearest fireplace. So, it was a surprise to Sister Agnes that a tumult was brewing in the freezing cold outside the abbey's portal.

Pulling her cloak about her, she left her work and, following the walkway from her workroom, past the chapel and out toward the portal, she sought the reason for the tumult. She stopped abruptly when a novice, rushing in the opposite direction, ran into her.

Sister Agnes – The First Confrontation

"Slow your steps, child," Agnes said firmly, steadying the girl. "Why are you running? You know well that we walk with reverence—never like startled cats."

"It is the intruders, Sister! A great throng stands at the gate. They cry out against something called *The Kindred* — shouting that the ones they seek are hiding within our walls!"

Agnes's brows drew together. "How many are they?"

"Many, Sister. More than there be sisters in the abbey!"

"Then walk, child—walk, I say—and fetch Mother Alice. Tell her what has come to pass. And make haste."

The novice started off at a run.

"Not *that* kind of haste, child!" Agnes called after her. "She will yet be there when you arrive, if you walk with purpose."

Turning once more toward the portal, Agnes reached the gate and found the sister posted there already embattled with the commotion.

"What be the trouble here, Sister?"

The gatekeeper, face drawn with worry, replied, "A crowd does press against the portal, Sister Agnes. They will not turn away. They cry that *The Kindred* dwell within and demand that we surrender them. I know not what truth lies behind their words. Worse still, some of our youngest novices and lay sisters have gone out into the cold to confront them. I fear this may turn to violence."

At that moment, Mother Alice arrived, her countenance set with quiet resolve. "Sister Agnes, what is the cause of this unrest?"

Agnes inclined her head. "A mob, Mother, demanding we hand over members of *The Kindred*. But there are none such within these walls, I swear it. Our novices and lay sisters, stirred by fear or defiance, have gone out to speak with them. We must call them back ere harm befalls them."

Mother Alice drew her heavy woolen cloak tight about her shoulders. Though she longed to remain within the warmth of the cloister, she walked without hesitation to the portal, which the posted sister opened without a word. Quietly, she stepped into the chill morning air and approached the cluster of young women.

"Return to your chambers. At once."

Her voice was low, but its authority was unquestionable. "Yes, Reverend Mother." The girls bowed their heads and, without protest, slipped back through the gate as it opened for them. Mother Alice did not watch them go. She turned instead to face the crowd.

The rabble surged, angry and loud, waving rakes, staffs, and pitchforks. Their shouts filled the air:

"We want *The Kindred*—now!"

"Give them to us, that they may be punished!"

"They stole my cow and slit its throat! Devil-worshippers, they be! They must hang or burn!"

Mother Alice raised her voice, calm yet unwavering. "There are no *Kindred* within these walls. Why say you that we harbour them?"

A voice cried out, "We know they be here, Mother! Word has come to us. Now turn them over and be quick about it!"

Her eyes swept the crowd. "Who leads this rabble?"

A tall man stepped forward—broad of shoulder, clean of face, and plainly but well-dressed.

"It be me, Mother."

She met his gaze with iron steadiness. "Then send these folk back to their homes and attend me. You shall speak your tale plainly, and you shall speak it true—if you care at all for your immortal soul."

Without waiting for his reply, she turned and stepped back toward the gate.

Mother Alice – The Leader of the Rabble

Mother Alice and Sister Agnes withdrew to the abbess's chambers to await the leader of the rabble. They had not long to wait. A sister who had stood watch at the portal during the commotion escorted the man into Mother Alice's presence.

He entered with a quiet confidence, his posture straight, his eyes steady. Though simply dressed, there was care in his appearance — garments neat, boots clean, long hair combed back from his brow. He met their gaze with something between pride and defiance, and waited to be addressed. "What is your name, sir?" asked Mother Alice.

"I be called Godfrey atte Welle, Mother."

"Well then, sit you down, Godfrey atte Welle, and speak your tale. Who be these folk you bring to our abbey, and to what end?"

"These be honest townsfolk, Mother—plain, yet good. We have heard tell that on All Hallows' Eve, you and your nuns did battle with *The Kindred*, who sacrificed a young girl to their foul gods. And, their bloody deed done, they fled and hid in the woods. Later, we heard, they came hither seeking sanctuary."

"All of that is false," said Sister Agnes, her brow furrowing. "No harm befell the girl of whom you speak. She was a novice of this house and has since returned to her family. The battle you refer to was not our doing, but that of Friar Thomas, *inquisitor in disciplina*, who came with soldiers of the pope's own guard, smuggled into Oxford months past for this particular purpose. None of *The Kindred* entered our cloisters, but Friar Thomas captured several; not, sadly, their leader." She turned to Mother Alice as if for confirmation.

The abbess nodded. "And so, Godfrey atte Welle, you will repair to your mob and tell them all that Sister Agnes has now told you, for it is truth, plainly and simply. Now leave us. Sister, escort Godfrey atte Welle to the gate.

"That I will, Mother, and gladly!" She left, leaving Mother Alice and Sister Agnes alone in the chambers.

Friar Thomas – Conspiracy

Friar Thomas entered Sister Agnes's workroom, a deep frown furrowing his brow. "There is unrest in the town, Sister. You yourself saw the mob that gathered at your gate, but yesterday. This turmoil is born of wicked rumours—tales that *The Kindred* sought sanctuary within these walls, and that Mother Alice granted it."

Agnes's eyes narrowed. "That is a lie, Friar. No member of *The Kindred* has ever set foot within our cloisters. Why does the undersheriff not put down these disturbances?"

Thomas shook his head. "I know not, Sister. Each time a fray erupts, the man is nowhere nearby."

Before he could say more, Alexis entered the chamber, her expression tense. "I have learned whence these rumours arise, Sister. There is a stranger—unknown to any in Oxford town—who comes to the Black Swan tavern and buys ale for all. As the drink flows, so do his tales, and the men lean in, eager for every word. He claims to have the sight."

Agnes looked sharply at her.

"Who is this man, Alexis?"

"I know not his full name, Friar," she replied, turning to Thomas, "but I can show you him. He is small of stature, lean and ragged in dress. He has long black hair falling loose and a beard untamed. His eyes burn with a strange light, and he carries a staff of yew. His name, whispered rarely, is Elias."

Friar Thomas's expression darkened.

"If he claims to be a seer, can you not confront him, Alexis? I will see to it that my men remain close at hand to ensure your safety."

"Aye, Friar. Since I bear the true sight, I shall ken at once whether his gift is false."

Mother Alice, who had entered unnoticed, nodded solemnly.

"So long as the friar's men guard you well, you have my leave. But go not in your own guise. Put on poor garb, lest he know you."

"That will I do, Mother. At once."

Alexis – Confrontation

Garbed in a tattered cloak and bearing a staff of ash—a symbol of the seer's gift, the power to see between worlds—Alexis made her way to the Black Swan tavern. Carved along the shaft in crude lines were ogham runes, an ancient script steeped in the mysticism of her Celtic blood.

Alexis strode through the tavern door. The fire crackled, and the low murmur of voices paused at her entry.

"What'll ye have, mistress?" the barmaid asked.

"Nothing, goodwife. I come not to drink, but to unmask a false seer." Her voice rang clear. Standing tall, her feet planted wide in challenge, she raised her staff and pointed it toward Elias.

"Speak, then, false prophet! If your sight be true, then name me. Who am I?"

A hush fell over the room. All eyes turned to Elias.

"I know not, mistress," he replied coolly. "But if you claim the Sight, then tell us—who am I?"

Alexis narrowed her eyes. Her voice, when it came, was low and steady. "You be Elias of Dunwode, and you be of *The Kindred*."

A gasp of disbelief swept through the tavern.

"Speaks she true?" a man cried. "Elias—are ye one of them?"

"I answer not to this sham seer," Elias spat. He drained the last of his ale in a single draught, seized his yew staff, and stalked from the tavern, his jaw clenched, his fury plain.

Godfrey atte Welle – Reconciliation

"Why does Godfrey atte Welle return to our abbey?" Mother Alice's tone showed her displeasure. "Did I not bid him depart?"

"Mother," said Sister Agnes, her voice calm and measured, "he comes to make amends for the conduct of the townsfolk."

The abbess sighed, fingers steepled before her. "Very well. Bid him enter, then."

Godfrey stepped into the chamber and bowed his head respectfully. "Mother. Sister. I come to offer my apologies for the townsfolk's behavior. Misled, we were, by one who called himself Elias—a false seer, and, we now believe, a servant of *The Kindred*. He spread lies, sowed discord, and turned us against this house unjustly.

"But no longer. The men of Oxford town are ready to make this right. I come to offer our strength—to aid you in rooting out these vermin and putting an end to their evil."

As he spoke, Friar Thomas entered the room. "I am grateful for your offer, Godfrey. But know this—we needs must work in close accord, and with utmost secrecy. Should *The Kindred* learn of our intent ere we act, all shall be for naught."

"There shall be no difficulty in that, Friar," Godfrey replied. "We shall keep our counsel close, and the townsmen shall know naught until the hour is ripe. What they know not, they cannot betray."

"Forsooth, Godfrey," the friar said, nodding approvingly.

At that moment, Isabel entered the chamber, her brow knit with worry. "Mother… there is trouble brewing within our walls. It touches many of our sisters, and I fear it shall bring ruin upon our reputation—and shatter the peace of our cloister."

Chapter 19
Shadows Within the Abbey

Suspicions grow among the nuns, with some accusing others of heresy or involvement, creating tension within the abbey, and complicating Agnes's effort, as well as vexing Mother Superior.

Isabel, what troubles you so, my child?" Mother Alice's gaze was steady as she waited for Isabel to answer.

"It is our sisters, Mother. They quarrel amongst themselves and cast blame, each accusing the other of harbouring The Kindred within our cloisters. But I know of no such evil dwelling here. How came they to think such things? They point fingers and speak of heresy."

Sister Agnes listened patiently, then raised a hand. "These be falsehoods, Isabel—lies sown by one of *The Kindred*, who posed as a seer in the town. Alexis confronted him in the Black Swan tavern, and he will trouble us no more. Yet how came these rumours to reach the ears of our sisters, who ne'er leave these walls?"

Isabel – Rumours in the Abbey

Isabel lowered her gaze. "Mayhap, Sister… mayhap one of the lay sisters who go into Oxford town to fetch provisions. Perchance they heard the whispers there and carried them back hither."

"And who among our sisters speaks loudest of these tales?"

"Sister Mary Magdalen, Sister. The others heed her, for she is oft quiet and contemplative. When such a one speaks, the rest give her words weight."

Mother Alice did not hesitate. "Then bring Sister Mary Magdalen hither, Isabel. Say to her that I would speak with her on a matter of great moment."

"Aye, Mother. At once."

It was not long before Isabel returned to the abbess's chambers, with Sister Mary Magdalen following close behind.

"Welcome, Sister," said Mother Alice gently. "I thank you for granting me a moment of your time."

"Gladly, Mother. If I may be of service, say but the word."

"You have heard the rumours of *The Kindred*—that they seek sanctuary within our walls?"

"Indeed, I have heard them," Mary Magdalen replied, her voice low yet fervent. "And I know well that some among us have aided them—welcomed them, even—that they might hide here and escape judgment. Such sisters are heretics, Mother! They do not belong within these hallowed walls."

She straightened, leveling her eyes on Mother Alice, her expression firm with resolve. "And, with respect, Mother, I shall hear no more of this blasphemy—until those heretics are gone. Now, by your leave, I shall return to my prayers... prayers for the salvation of all our immortal souls."

Without awaiting dismissal, she turned and departed, leaving Mother Alice, Sister Agnes, and Isabel staring after her, too stunned to speak.

Alexis – Chasing Rumours

"Isabel… go and fetch Alexis, I pray you."

"At once, Mother."

Puzzled, Sister Agnes turned to the abbess. "What can Alexis do for us, Mother?"

"She may find the lay sister—if lay sister it be—who has brought this false tale into the abbey. For Alexis is one of them, and she has the gift of discerning truth from falsehood."

Moments later, Alexis entered the abbess's chambers, a look of curiosity upon her face.

"Good day to you, Mother… Sister," she said with a respectful bow. "To what end have you summoned me hither?"

Mother Alice gestured for her to come closer. "Alexis, there are rumours abroad that we harbour members of *The Kindred*. They are false, of course, yet Sister Mary Magdalen believes them true, and she speaks it openly. We think, mayhap, that one of the lay sisters, sent into Oxford for provisions, heard such tales spread by the false seer and brought them back upon her return."

"We needs must know if this be so," Sister Agnes added. "And if it be, we must learn who has done this, that she may be called to account—and the harm she wrought made right."

"Mother… it be no lay sister. It be the sister herself."

"How can that be, Alexis? How came she by such rumours?"

"Recall, Mother, that Sister Mary Magdalen does journey to the university now and again to minister to the students and faculty. 'Tis there, I believe, she first heard these false tales."

"And how do you know this, Alexis?"

"She told me so, Mother. Ofttimes, she takes her meals in her chamber, and I am the one who brings them. She speaks, and I but listen. She said the tales, spoken oft at the university, which is a place where the false seer does most like to sow his wicked lies. The students, especially the younger lads, give ear to him and pass on his words without care. I ken that Sister Mary Magdalen did speak with one such youth… and believed him."

Mother Alice's expression grew dark. "Then I shall go to the sister myself. She has much to answer for."

Without another word, the abbess turned and departed for Sister Mary Magdalen's chamber.

Mother Alice – Confronting Sister Mary Magdalen

Mother Alice entered Sister Mary Magdalen's chamber without knocking, her visage shadowed with anger, though her voice remained low and measured.

"Sister, you have been spreading false rumours."

"I have done no such thing, Mother. The tales I spoke are true."

"How do you know this, Sister?"

"They be abroad in the town and at the university. The students I minister unto told me, and I believe they speak true."

"Yet you gave me no courtesy, no chance to explain how those tales are naught but falsehood. Instead, you did storm from my chambers in a manner most unbefitting your vows."

"The Adversary beguiles you, Mother. He would have you believe there is naught amiss within these cloistered walls. But I say to you—there is much amiss, and certain of our sisters do abet it."

"Mark me well, Sister. I shall tell you the truth, plain and full. If, after hearing it, you choose still to sow discord and speak falsehood, I shall have no choice but to expel you from Godstow Abbey. Do you understand me?"

Sister Mary Magdalen sat stiffly in her straight-backed wooden chair, her face composed, though her eyes betrayed a simmering defiance.

"Say on, Mother. You are, after all, our superior, and when you speak, we must hearken."

"Indeed, you must," said Mother Alice firmly. "For I speak with the authority not only of this abbey, but of our Holy Mother Church.

"These tales, Sister, contrived by a false seer, have spread with great swiftness and no little violence. Townsfolk did riot at our gate, speaking the selfsame words that you have repeated. Their leader, brought before me, did recount from whom and whence these tales arose. The seer is a known member of *The Kindred*, and his purpose is clear—to sow discord and confusion, that his heretical brethren might thrive unseen.

"It is true, as you have heard, that *The Kindred* did attempt a blood sacrifice of one of our novices. Yet by the grace of God, and the timely intervention of Friar Thomas—a man of the Inquisition and held in high regard by our Holy Father in Rome—the girl escaped. His men, drawn from the personal guard of our pope, fell upon the ritual as it neared its vile conclusion. The archdruid had not yet brought his blade to the novice's throat when they intervened. Alas, the archdruid escaped into the wood, and his identity remains unknown to us.

"Many of *The Kindred* did scatter, but the men-at-arms captured not a few. Yet let it be known: *not one of them sought sanctuary within these walls*. And had they, I would not have granted it.

"This be the truth, Sister Mary Magdalen. Now shall you go to those sisters whom your words have troubled and stirred, and you shall tell them the truth as I have spoken it. And when next the confessor visits our abbey, you shall make full confession of your part in spreading these false rumours and accept with humility the penance he shall assign you. Do you understand me, Sister?"

This was a bitter pill for the nun, a long-time member of the cloistered community. Her eyes, still smoldering with defiance, belied her soft answer. "Yes, Mother. I shall tell our sisters the tale as you related it. And I shall confess my part in spreading these rumours. But it remains that *The Kindred* and their leader are still abroad."

"You speak true, Sister, and Friar Thomas is doing all that he may to stop them, force them to scatter and capture their leader. Now I will leave you to your prayers. I suggest that you ask the Blessed Virgin Mary and Saint Mary Magdalen, your patroness, to give you the strength you will need to quell this disturbance in our sacred abbey."

"Such will I do, Mother, but not gladly."

Chapter 20

A Demon's Rite

In which the reality of heathen worship and its ties to the abbey come to light, revealing a splintered sect with divided allegiances to conflicting deities. An important member of the sect dies in the battle between the sect's two factions.

Sir Edwin de Ravenswold had grown weary of the violence and bloodshed that marked *The Kindred's* observance of the feast days. The failed sacrifice of the novice, Cecily, lingered in his thoughts and vexed him sorely, even as the spring equinox drew nigh, now but five months hence.

Though *The Kindred* had, in large part, scattered and gone into hiding, Sir Edwin de Ravenswold knew well that among their number were those who longed for a gentler path—a worship quiet and reverent, rooted in the rhythms of nature. With Celtic and Druidic bloodlines stretching across time and the Irish Sea, Edwin yearned to return to the ancient ways of his forebears, to the sacred grounds on the Isle of Man, where, in earlier days, Druids paid homage to nature, to the horned god Cernunnos, and to the radiant earth-mother Brigid.

The spring equinox—*Feailley ny Craaghyn* (the Festival of the Trees, in the Manx tongue)—spoke of rebirth, as winter's icy hold yielded to budding trees, flowering hedgerows, and the stirring of new life among the wild creatures of field and forest. Edwin's thoughts turned to such rites—peaceful, sacred, and far removed from the blood-soaked altars of *The Kindred*.

Lady Beatrix – Letter to Lady Harriet

Frown lines creased the brow of Lady Beatrix de Aylesbridge. Warned away from Sir Edwin by her trusted friend Sister Agnes, by Professor Barrington, and even her cousin Eleanor, she found herself in painful doubt. His words to her, spoken months past beneath the crisp night sky, had rung with warmth and trust. Yet when she turned to answer him, he had vanished into the night.

Since that time, a letter had come from Eleanor—implying, nay, stating outright—that Edwin had once consorted with *The Kindred*. That he might have played a part in the failed Samhain sacrifice of the novice Cecily was beyond all imagining. And yet…

She recalled the counsel of Sister Agnes, offered in the quiet of her workroom: *Seek the counsel of trusted friends, such as Lady Harriet.* At once, she took up parchment and a quill and wrote a letter to Lady Harriet FitzAlan.

> *My dear Lady Harriet,*
> *May I have the honor of a visit from you on the*
> *morrow? Come in the early afternoon—we shall*
> *take tea, and I crave your advice.*
> *Your affectionate friend,*
> *Lady Beatrix de Aylesbridge*

She folded the letter, sealed it with green wax, and pressed her family's crest-ring deep into the warm seal.

Summoning her steward, she handed it to him. "See that this reaches Lady Harriet FitzAlan with all haste. Tarry not—it is of the utmost moment."

"Aye, My Lady. It shall be as you desire."

It was later in the afternoon of the next day when the footman entered the library of de Aylesbridge Manor. "My Lady, Lady Harriet stands without the door, awaiting your pleasure."

"Do bid her enter. I have long anticipated her visit."

"As you will, My Lady."

Moments later, Lady Harriet stepped into the grand library, a chamber lined with shelves of books and adorned with oil portraits and marble statuary. The high ceiling and paneled walls echoed with the quiet refinement typical of such manor houses. At a carved mahogany writing table sat Lady Beatrix, mulling over Eleanor's letter and recalling past counsel from Sister Agnes and Professor Barrington.

"My dear Harriet," she rose to greet her guest, "how glad I am to see you. I shall ring for tea—and perhaps some small cakes?"

"Indeed, Beatrix, I came gladly, and naught would have kept me away. Tea and cakes sound delightful."

"Good." Beatrix reached for the ornate bell cord by the tall double doors. A moment later, the steward appeared.

"Kindly ask Cook to prepare a tray—cakes and a pot of tea, two cups."

"At once, My Lady."

Harriet seated herself opposite her hostess. "Now, Beatrix, how may I help you?"

"I find myself in torment over Sir Edwin. Word has come that he consorts with *The Kindred*… but I cannot reconcile that with the man I thought I knew. He is not one to raise a blade against a helpless girl. He is gentle. He is kind."

"Then why not confront him?" Harriet asked simply.

"He does not answer my letters."

"Then go to him," Harriet said firmly. "Do not wait upon his reply. Ride to his manor and put your questions to him directly. Accept no evasions. And if he will not answer you… that, in itself, is an answer. Tell me, Beatrix, what truly do you know of his past? Of his family? Have you sought that out?"

Beatrix sighed. "Little enough, I fear. Only that his is an old family, but one whispered of in dark tales."

At that moment, the steward returned, bearing a silver tray with tea and cakes. He placed it with practiced care upon the table and withdrew.

"You speak with wisdom, as always," said Beatrix, preparing to pour the tea. "Your counsel is sound and ever gladdens my heart. I shall do as you suggest."

"Then I am content," Harriet smiled. "Now… shall we enjoy this tea?"

"Of course, Harriet. I'll pour."

The remainder of the afternoon passed in quiet warmth and pleasant conversation. Beatrix, her course now clear, set her doubts aside—at least for the moment—and turned her thoughts to sweeter things.

Lady Beatrix – Edwin's Tale

The new day dawned warm and fair. Spring, at last, was in the air. In the early afternoon light, birds sang cheerily, and small creatures stirred upon the broad lawns of the de Aylesbridge estate. Lady Beatrix summoned her steward.

"Bid the groom ready my carriage and fetch my footman. I would go to Ravenswold."

"At once, My Lady."

The ride to Ravenswold was not brief, but Beatrix made good use of the time. She gazed out upon the greening countryside, where trees unfurled new leaves and early blooms touched the hedgerows with color. A soft breeze blew from the west, bearing the sweet breath of flowers, lifting her spirits even as it stirred her unease.

This visit, should Edwin grant it, promised to be no easy meeting. She had questions—hard ones—that she needs must ask, no matter the pain they might cause. His silence these many months, his sudden departure that night, and, most of all, the whispered warnings from Agnes and the professor weighed heavy on her heart.

As the carriage neared Ravenswold Hall, a stately and many-chambered manor of grey stone nestled near Cumnor at the edge of the Cotswold forests, the road grew rough with the remnants of spring rains and snowmelt. Even so, the journey had taken but a few hours.

Her doubts, however, arrived with her. *What if he should turn me away?* she wondered. *What shall I do then?*

But it was too late to question. Her footman was already down, reaching to assist her from the carriage, guiding her to the massive doors that guarded the secrets of Ravenswold.

With hesitant hands, she knocked—softly, then with greater resolve—upon the great door. It opened slowly with a long groan of wood and iron. A steward, stooped with age, his thinning white hair drawn back, regarded her with weary eyes.

"Yes, My Lady? How may I serve you?"

"I would speak with Sir Edwin," she said, her tone firm, more strident than she had intended. "And I shall brook no delay."

The steward gave a courteous bow. "And who shall I say seeks him, My Lady? Please, enter and await here in the entry hall. I shall ask my master if he would grant you audience."

"I am Lady Beatrix de Aylesbridge. He knows me well. My errand is of great import, so I bid you make haste."

"Aye, My Lady. At once."

The old man disappeared down a dim corridor, his gait slow but sure. Within but a few moments he returned.

"My master will receive you, My Lady. This way, if you please."

Beatrix followed him through the long corridor until at last he opened a pair of carved wooden doors, revealing a chamber that took her breath.

It was the largest library she had ever seen in a manor house.

The carved ceiling soared high above, forest scenes with strange creatures painted upon it, enclosing three lofty levels of shelves, each crowded with books, scrolls, and manuscripts, some ancient, their bindings worn with time. Parchment and vellum alike piled in orderly stacks upon the floor, and niches in the walls held statues— gods and goddesses of unfamiliar design, some serene, others wild-eyed. Portraits hung here and there in the gaps between shelves— grim visages of long-dead men and women who bore, in subtle ways, the look of Edwin.

But nowhere did she spy weaponry, nor did any grotesque demon stare back from canvas or carving. The dimly lit chamber felt... *curious*, not evil. Its mystery invited questions, not fear.

She drew in a steadying breath and waited.

From behind a great oaken desk, intricately carved with ancient symbols and crests long forgotten, Edwin rose. He did not step forward to greet her but met her gaze with a guarded solemnity.

"Why come you here, My Lady?" he asked, voice low and strained. "Did you not know that my silence these many months past meant that I would not see you?"

"That is my first question, Edwin," she replied, her voice steady though her heart raced. "Why?"

"Please, Beatrix," he said, gesturing. "Be seated, and I shall give you answers."

She moved toward the large, cushioned chair set across from his desk.

"Nay," he added gently, "not there. Let us sit by the fire. Though spring has come to the land, these stones hold the winter chill. This hall, built many generations past for strength, not comfort, traps the cold in its ancient walls for some time."

They moved to the hearth, where two well-worn but noble chairs faced one another on either side of the flame. The fire crackled softly, casting flickers of gold upon the walls.

Edwin waited until they sat before he spoke again.

"I did not wish to see you," he said at last, "because I love you. And to be near you again is to place you in peril. You and your friends at Godstow… you dig too near the root of the truth. The Archdruid is aware of this, and it vexes him greatly. When he is angered, he does not forgive. He kills."

Beatrix sat in thoughtful silence for a time, weighing his words. It was not the first time he had professed love for her, and perhaps this was the best answer she could hope for. She chose to accept it — for now.

"There is more I would know, Edwin. I would know of your past, your ancestors, your family."

Edwin gazed at the fire as if deciding what more to say. Or, mayhap, how to tell his story that she might understand. Finally, with a low voice, he started.

"Where stone walls stand and chapel bells ring out on the Isle of Man, there once was a sacred grove. The oak and ash stood tall where the fortress walls now rise, and the wind off the sea sang the names of the Old Gods. Before the Norsemen's longships, before the church and the crypt with the bones beneath it, the land was holy in a quieter way. The roots went deep.

"My bloodline traces to those who gathered there—keepers of the sacred fire, and of the old songs and truths spoken long before ever they were writ. My ancestors were Druids—not warriors seeking power but guides who lived in harmony with the land. Their strength came from communion, not conquest. They honored Brigid, goddess of healing and hearth. They listened, they learned, they tended the balance between people and the spirits that dwell in earth, sea, and sky. They read the stars and spoke with the stones. But over time, we became few, and in the shadow of new kings and new faiths, we hid our rites beneath silence and symbol."

"But how came you to consort with such as *The Kindred*? Surely, if I am to believe you, they do not speak with the same voice that you describe."

"*The Kindred…* they claimed to preserve what we had lost, but they twisted the old ways. They profaned our rites. Blood and shadow in place of balance and blessing. Power without reverence. The Archdruid—I walked with him once. Now he feeds the flame with cruelty.

"I broke with them. I walked away from the hollow thunder of their chants—noise without spirit, power without purpose. I have returned to the roots, to the quiet truths buried beneath their blood rites. *The Circle of the Old Grove* —scattered though we may be—

we remember. And we will restore the lost traditions. Not through force and fear, but by reviving what was sacred and forgotten.

"I am the last of my line, Beatrix. But the line breaks not if the fire passes from generation to generation. The old ways are not dead. They sleep. And in time, they shall wake."

Edwin stared into the fire as though its dancing flames transported him away from Ravenswold Hall and back across the sea to his Manx ancestors, back to the Druids who guarded the sacred bond between humankind and the natural world; Druids whose gods and goddesses were noble, kind, and loving. Beatrix sat in silent contemplation for a time. This was not the Edwin she had come to fear. This was Edwin de Ravenswold, stripped of the violent legends that had dogged his name through the ages—Edwin de Ravenswold, descendant of nobles, of Druids, and their gentle deities. *Her* Edwin de Ravenswold.

Edwin – Confrontation

Later, Edwin mounted his midnight-black rouncey and rode toward the forest on the edge of his lands. Dressed to make an impression, his bearing regal as he approached the circle where *The Kindred* was gathering.

At the center, near a blazing bonfire, stood the Archdruid. The symbolic sword of his office was clutched tightly in one hand, and at his feet lay an arbalest.

"What brings you to our gathering, Sir Edwin de Ravenswold?" the Archdruid snarled. "You are not welcome here. Go back to your 'Circle of the Old Grove' and whisper to your weak gods and goddesses. We have no use for hollow men such as you who kneel to fading gods."

In the shadows, hidden among the trees beyond the firelight, stood Beatrix. Silent. Watching. Unseen and unknown to Edwin, she strained to glimpse the face of the Archdruid, but his features concealed behind a gruesome mask revealed nothing.

"Master Archdruid," Edwin's voice rang clear across the firelit glade, "what you do here is blasphemy—in the eyes of the Church, and in the eyes of *The Circle*. I come to end your violence… with one final act."

He drew his longsword—a heavy, ancient blade, forged in antiquity by the hands of his ancestors. Gripping the hilt in both hands, he raised it before him.

"This night, you shall die, Archdruid. You shall ply your bloody rites no more."

Gasps echoed through the assembled *Kindred* at Edwin's defiance—he had challenged the one they deemed immortal. The Archdruid cast down his obsidian blade and reached for the arbalest, leveling it with grim purpose. His finger curled upon the tickler.

From the woods, Beatrix rushed forward, shouting, "You shall not kill Edwin, you fiend! Put down your weapon. Leave this place and save your life!"

"You!" the Archdruid roared. "It is *you* who turned this knight against his brethren. You who whispered poison into his ear, weakening him with talk of love. You shall die before him!"

Sarcastic and cruel, he swung the arbalest toward her. Beatrix froze as his finger tightened.

Before the bolt could fly, Edwin moved—swift and sure— placing himself between her and the deadly bow. The last thing he heard before the bolt struck home was the *zing* of the arbalest string. The quarrel pierced his chest, and Edwin de Ravenswold fell at Beatrix's feet.

Beatrix dropped to her knees. "You must not leave me, Edwin. My world ends without you." She cradled his head in her lap, blood spilling onto her velvet gown, staining it deep crimson.

"It is over, Beatrix," he whispered. "I will wait for you in the next world, where we shall love for eternity. Just… hold me."

And then he was gone.

Beatrix bowed her head, her tears falling upon the black cloak embroidered with the silver ravens, as grief overcame her.

Suddenly, the forest erupted with the sound of hooves and shouting. Friar Thomas's men had arrived. *The Kindred* scattered into the trees, and as before, the Archdruid disappeared into the night.

Friar Thomas dismounted at once. Seeing Edwin's lifeless body, he summoned two of his men.

"Bear him home," he said softly.

The men-at-arms lifted Edwin with care, laying him across a riderless horse. Slowly, reverently, they carried him back to Ravenswold Hall.

Chapter 21
A Search Through Old Evidence

In which Agnes, Isabel, Beatrix, and Alexis examine evidence from five years prior, guided by newer clues only recently brought to light. Together, these revelations unveil a pattern of deception and manipulation, suggesting that The Kindred planned Cecily's indoctrination into the sect long in advance.

Sister Agnes sat in her workroom with Isabel, Lady Beatrix, and Alexis. She leaned forward, a frown of concern on her face, as she mulled over the events of recent days. Something, she knew, did not sit right.

"Does it not seem," she began slowly, "that Cecily was far more deeply entangled with *The Kindred* than we had first believed?"

"Sister," Lady Beatrix replied, her voice thoughtful, "I have had much the same notion. It struck me she was far too familiar with their ways—almost as if she had known them since she first came to Godstow, these five years gone."

Isabel leaned forward, her brow drawn. "In those years, there were strange occurrences we never could explain. We took them for accidents or idle mischief. But now, in light of what has since unfolded, they seem of far greater weight. Yet still, their cause remains hidden from us.

Alexis spoke, her voice low but firm. "Something troubles me, Sister. What if there are others like Cecily still within our cloisters? Friar Thomas believed heresy dwelt among us—perchance he spoke the truth. Some may have been here for a long while, and we simply do not see them for what they are."

Sister Agnes – A New Resolve

Agnes nodded solemnly. "Aye, you speak true. We must find out the whole of it."

Lady Beatrix looked uncertain. "But how are we to uncover such truths, Sister? Some of these events lie five years in the past."

"We needs must return to that time, My Lady," Agnes replied. "Not in body, but in thought. We shall sift through old records, speak with those who were present, and seek patterns where before we saw none. If the evidence mounts high enough, then perchance, we shall have our answer."

Isabel began, "She came to us six years past. Her parents brought her when she was but fourteen, a tender age, yet already given to mischief and consorting with the university boys, most of them older than she. By the next year, she began to take up small tasks within the abbey. Then, or so the rumours tell, she became infatuated with Martin— the rugged stable hand with a dangerous charm about him. Do you recall that, Sister?"

"Forsooth, I do," Agnes replied gravely. "It was about that same time that pages vanished from my copy of the *Picatrix*. That I recall most vividly[2]:

> *Her fragment of the Picatrix, an 11th-century treatise on astrological magic containing arcane,*

---

2 See <u>The Whispering Dead of Rewley Abbey</u>, the first book in the "Murder in the Abbey" series, chapter 22.

occult knowledge, was not in its usual resting place.

The sections "A Deadly Poison" and "Another Deadly Poison" had been roughly torn from the volume. She browsed further and found that another section, one which she had referred to in the past, "A Theriac for Every Poison" was, likewise, missing. This was a cure for all types of poisoning.

"I thought, at the time, that it was but a prank—or perchance one of the sisters, fearful of such an arcane manuscript dwelling within our cloisters, removed the pages.

"Now, I am no longer certain."

At that moment, Mother Alice entered the workroom.

"Good day to you, Mother," Agnes greeted her. "We are much concerned about Cecily. We fear there may be others of her ilk yet among us."

"I share your concerns, Sister. Forsooth, it is that fear which brings me hither. Though it has been six months since Cecily departed our community, her chamber remains untouched. All lies as she left it, her writings, her habits, her other garments— and some strange manuscripts we cannot decipher. It would be well if you and your companions examined her chamber. Perchance therein lie some clues to aid your inquiry. You also might seek aid from the professor to understand that strange manuscript."

"We shall fetch the manuscripts and anything else of interest, Mother." With that, Agnes, Beatrix, Isabel, and Alexis made their way to Cecily's chamber.

Sister Agnes – Cecily's Chamber

Sister Agnes, Isabel, Beatrix, and Alexis entered the narrow cell once occupied by Cecily.

"Mother was correct, Sister," Beatrix said quietly. "This room is in considerable disarray."

"So it be, My Lady. So it be."

From a shadowed corner, Alexis called out, "Look you, Sister! Yon wooden coffer—mayhap it holds something useful."

Beatrix crossed to the coffer. It was old, worn smooth by years of use, the wood scarred, and the iron lock rusted with age. "Isabel… fetch your key. Let us see if it opens this."

"Certainly, My Lady." Isabel hurried off and returned with her key. Beatrix tried it in the ancient lock, but it did not turn.

Agnes, standing by the small writing table, sifted through the clutter. Under a sheet of vellum, she spied a key—duller and heavier than most. "Try you this one, My Lady."

Beatrix took the key, inserted it, and twisted. With a loud, grinding *click*, the lock gave way. She lifted the lid.

"Look you, all—there are documents aplenty here. These are the missing pages from the *Picatrix*. And here… these must be the pages written in the strange tongue that Mother spoke of. She must have opened the coffer and relocked it to keep the contents safe."

Agnes stepped forward and carefully gathered the parchments. "Wait, here is something more. Dried herbs, long dead but still pungent. I believe these may be the herbs we found growing in the garden—forbidden, dangerous ones."

"Hold, Alexis! Touch them not," she cautioned. "My Lady, have you a kerchief or wrapping wherein we may safely convey these to my workroom?"

Beatrix reached for her pouch and produced a square of linen. Gingerly, she wrapped the herbs and tucked them away.

Meanwhile, Isabel bent over the writing table. "Sister! My Lady! Alexis! Come see what I have found!" she cried. "A confession—in Cecily's own hand! She tells all!"

Agnes took the page, her eyes scanning the lines. "Aye, Isabel. This shall guide the rest of our inquiries. Mother certainly will wish to see this."

Six years ago, I was sent to the nunnery. Throughout that time, I was secretly wth The Kindred and I regret it deeply.
Prior to coming to Godstow, I kept company with the University boys. After I came to the abbey, I kept company with Martin, the stable hand. One year after arriving, I stole pages from the Picatrix and gave them to The Kindred. After I was made a novice, I spied on the abbey and told The Kindred of the secret names of God. Last week, I was present at The Kindred's blasphemous rite at the fire pit.
Now I have left the abbey and am going home.

Cecily Fuller

1 November 1299

Sister Agnes – Mother Alice

Sister Agnes walked with hurried gait to the abbess's chambers. "Mother, you must see what we found in Cecily's chamber. Here is the most important page that we found there." And she placed Cecily's confession on the worktable at which Mother Alice sat.

"Forsooth, Sister, this, indeed, is a treasure. We now can answer our questions. And we know from this that there is at least one of *The Kindred* among us."

"Aye, Mother. Martin, the stable hand, certainly is one of their brethren. We must rid ourselves of him at once. Perhaps the undersheriff will take him in hand and see to justice.

Look you at these other pages. Some are from my *Picatrix*, torn out these five years hence. Her confession says that she gave them to *The Kindred*, but they must have returned them to her after they copied them into their own book. See you… the torn edges of the pages for cert will match my book, from where they came."

The abbess examined the pages carefully.

De Venenis Lethalibus

De mortiferorum venenum
confocdicit. Virtus in herbis
multis et mineralosis periculo-
sis conficiuntur. los parinios
repenant contratas prasmittis
formosa rimanuior morbis.
Venena mortiferorum mistica
vintant. Indem autem venena
in corpus intravit. Quaratium
morbodo abera organisnus
furrescit. ris versum puis. puis
cui in de oircur puruscertum.
Etiant, in proba ridicen, liquis
vitae labonum mollitas arcu.

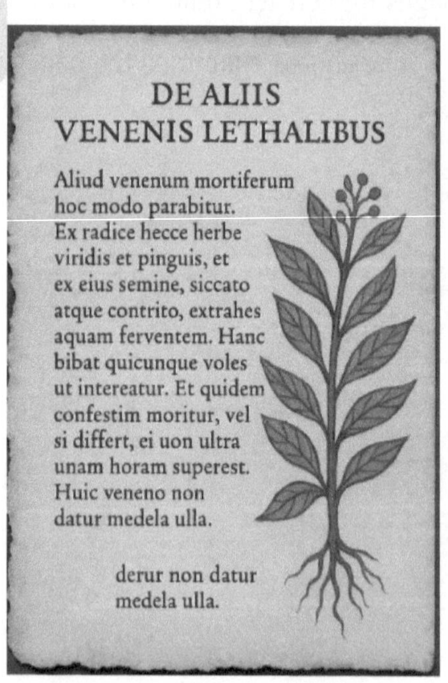

DE ALIIS VENENIS LETHALIBUS

Aliud venenum mortiferum
hoc modo parabitur.
Ex radice hecce herbe
viridis et pinguis, et
ex eius semine, siccato
atque contrito, extrahes
aquam ferventem. Hanc
bibat quicunque voles
ut intereatur. Et quidem
confestim moritur, vel
si differt, ei uon ultra
unam horam superest.
Huic veneno non
datur medela ulla.

derur non datur
medela ulla.

THERIACA AD
UNIVERSA VENENORUM

Quanda pheretatiis coer puiditum ultraque vina. Drachma forma tuet dépriscerrat potiserant, exterbi vine ultraque vio accra ifupa. Serifrigeriuor panices jvine, uEde átæ effecaiut, malem annostiis animo. Vine healitant um form equate poficu enorime vina aut vine mixta de. Leaf de rue toequies facfilitura allias signis. Saxifrigam antidotur pa tutt veneona. Leaf of rue e vine aut tutta ant toa alli zeiconas per touttalias venenone videm cidotur afcolquenosa. Mueca nima xpira antidotum utute dubare.

Agnes explained. "The first two refer to deadly poisons and other antidotes for deadly poisons. The third describes theriacs that can counter any poison. These descriptions match deadly herbs that we found in our garden this autumn past and which we now have found in the coffer in Cecily's chamber."

"And what of the strange writing? Do you know what it means?"

"Nay, Mother. I know not. That is a task for the professor. However, I do know that this is *The Kindred's* book of ritual. It is a book of dark magic, rituals – including blood sacrifices, one of which we witnessed already – chants and prayers to infernal demons and dark angels. These pages, which we found in Cecily's coffer, appear to speak of the making of poisons from baneful herbs."

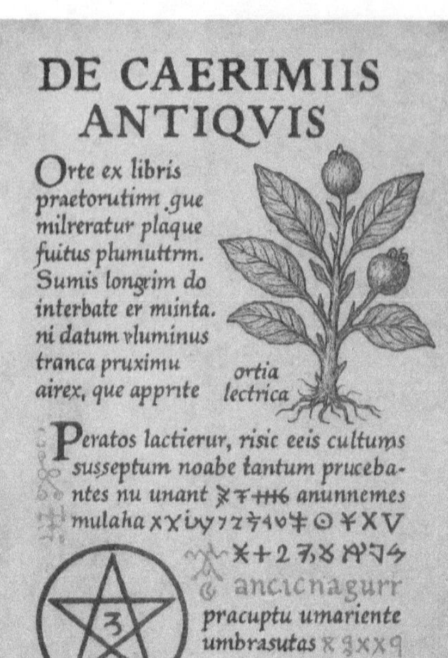
DE CAERIMIIS
ANTIQVIS
Orte ex libris
praetorutim gue
milreratur plaque
fuitus plumuttrm.
Sumis longrim do
interbate er miinta.
ni datum vluminus
tranca pruximu
airex, que apprite
ortia
lectrica
Peratos lactierur, risic eeis cultums
susseptum noabe tantum pruceba-
ntes nu unant anunnemes
mulaha

Codex Arcana

"Very well, Sister. We shall summon the professor once more. Mayhap he can translate these pages for us. See you to getting word to him that, again, his services be sore needed."

"Aye, Mother. So I shall. At once.

Sister Agnes – The Professor

Professor Barrington entered Sister Agnes's workroom with quiet deference. "A very good day to you, Sister. How may I be of service? I presume your summons pertains, once again, to *The Kindred*?"

"Forsooth, Professor. Indeed, it does. We searched Cecily's chamber and found these pages, written in a strange hand. Might you divine their meaning?"

The professor took the folios in hand, examining them closely. From time to time, he borrowed Agnes's magnifying stone, peering with intensity at the faded script and symbols.

"These pages are old, but not ancient," he said at last. "They are penned in a mixture of Latin and an unknown tongue—possibly ciphered or constructed. The content refers, unmistakably, to poisonous herbs, but also includes astrological symbols and alchemical diagrams."

He held the parchment up to the light. "These are excerpted from a notorious grimoire of infernal craft known as the *Codex Arcana*— sometimes called the *Codex Obscura*. I daresay Cecily could not read the unknown tongue, but the Latin alone would have sufficed. It speaks clearly of gathering, cultivating, and refining baneful herbs into lethal tinctures."

Agnes frowned. "We also uncovered a copy of the Samhain ritual from that same book. Could Cecily have had the entire *Codex*, do you think? Or did we recover only a fragment?"

"It is possible, Sister, but unlikely. I suspect she possessed only select pages—perhaps gifted by the Archdruid himself. They were likely sufficient to teach her what he intended… enough to cause the illnesses that plagued your sisters."

Agnes nodded gravely. "There is one more thing, Professor. We found Cecily's *Book of Hours*, but its margins bear disturbing scribbles. Heretical ideas. Praise for the 'Old Ones.'"

The professor straightened slightly. "Have you the book with you, Sister? I may learn more from it than mere handwriting."

"Forsooth, we do." Agnes passed it to him with care.

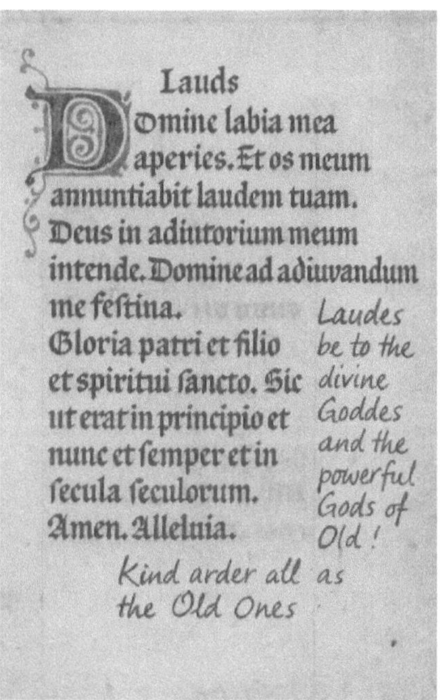

Agnes retrieved the book and placed it gently into Professor Barrington's hands. "It is, as you see, a standard *Book of Hours*, Professor. This page bears the prayer for Lauds—see here."

Domine, labia mea aperies. Et os meum
annuntiabit laudem tuam.
Deus in adiutorium meum intende. Domine ad
adiuvandum me festina.
Gloria Patri, et Filio, et Spiritui Sancto. Sic ut erat
in principio, et nunc, et semper, et in saecula
saeculorum. Amen.
Alleluia.

*(O Lord, open my lips. And my mouth shall
proclaim your praise.*

*O God, come to my assistance. O Lord, make
haste to help me.
Glory be to the Father, and to the Son, and to the
Holy Spirit. As it was in the beginning, is now, and
ever shall be, world without end. Amen.
Alleluia.)"*

"What is troubling, Professor, is the note in the margin:

*"Lauds be to the divine goddess and the powerful
Gods of Old! Kind arder all as the Old Ones."*

"I must confess that I can make nothing of it."

"Let me look at it a bit more closely, Sister. The strange wording suggests that she was under the influence of some herb or incense— perhaps a baneful one known to dull the senses and summon visions. While I cannot be certain, this is what it may mean:

*Lauds be to the divine goddess and the powerful
Gods of Old!*

Kind ardor.

All is of the will of the Old Ones.

"She writes, it seems, a hymn of praise to the old gods. She gives herself more to *The Kindred* than to Holy Church. You said Alexis and Isabel caught her burning pages from her Book? Mayhap they bore like words—perhaps this very text—and she cast them into the flames as an offering to the Old Ones."

"Indeed, they might, Professor. And there may be others of her ilk within these cloistered walls."

Chapter 22
Web of Deceit

In which Sister Agnes, Isabel, Alexis, and Lady Beatrix attempt to piece together the splintered sect's power dynamics and motives. Suspicions grow within the abbey, and the undersheriff brings a few key members of The Kindred to justice, revealing the inner conflict between the followers of Astaroth and Brigid. Questionable testimony from a suspected sect member.

Lady Beatrix was struck with grief beyond words at Edwin's death, for only days before, his gallant act had saved her life, and in that moment, she had come to know the true depth of his character. In the soft light of spring's early days, they had at last spoken openly of their love and of the hopes that might yet lie before them. But now he was gone.

Still, there were matters unsettled.

From within her writing desk, Beatrix drew forth the letter Edwin had written before his final confrontation. Witnessed and signed by his loyal steward, Godwin atte Hall, and by Father Osmund, chaplain of Ravenswold, Edwin named her the lawful custodian and guardian of his estates, to serve in his name until such time as a rightful heir of his blood might claim the title:

<u>To whom this present writing shall come,</u>

Know that I, Sir Edwin de Ravenswold, knight and rightful lord of Ravenswold Hall, being of sound mind and in fear that death may come upon me in these troubled days, do set forth this writing to make known my will.

Let it be known that it is my intent, solemn and true, to take to wife Lady Beatrix de Aylesbridge, noblewoman of worthy house and unblemished virtue. The matter of our union declared and agreed betwixt us, witnessed in private by my trusted steward, Godwin atte Hall, and the household chaplain, Father Osmund.

Should death or mischance befall me ere the bonds of matrimony are made, I do name and appoint the Lady Beatrix to be the custodian and guardian of all my lands and household at Ravenswold, to hold the same in my name, until such time as a rightful heir of my blood, if any there be, may claim his or her birthright.

All retainers and servants of my house shall render obedience and fealty to her in this charge, and no claim recognized above hers save by writ of His Grace, the King.

Given this on the Vigil of Saint Benedict, in the Year of Our Lord thirteen hundred, with mine own hand and seal, in the hall of Ravenswold.

Sir Edwin de Ravenswold [Seal of Sir Edwin de Ravenswold]

Witnessed this day by me,
Godwin atte Hall, steward of Ravenswold Hall

and

Father Osmund, Chaplain

That she now held charge over the de Ravenswold holdings was certain. But what troubled her most was the question of the future. Could there truly be an heir?

And more than that, there was the matter of *The Circle*, the gentle sect Edwin had initiated in contrast to *The Kindred's* darkness. She had seen its purity, its reverence for the old ways unmarred by blood or cruelty. But how would Sister Agnes respond, were she to learn that Beatrix had consorted with a sect that called upon heathen gods, no matter how peaceful its intent?

Lady Beatrix – Sister Agnes

"My thanks to you, Sister," Beatrix began, her voice low. "It is no light errand that brings me hither, and I crave your wisdom."

Agnes inclined her head. "If I may offer counsel, My Lady, you shall have it."

Beatrix drew in a breath. "I shall speak plain. Sir Edwin laboured to bring down *The Kindred*, for he deemed them cruel and their gods naught but devils from the Pit. In that, he served righteousness. He gave his life to spare mine. I cannot turn from his cause. I needs must continue what he began."

Agnes listened, grave of face.

"I know full well," Beatrix continued, "that this work sets me against the will of Mother Church. Yet I say this, Sister: the gods of *The Circle* be not the foul beings served by *The Kindred*. *The Circle* honours Brigid, goddess of the hearth and healing—she is not unlike Saint Brigid of Kildare, whose flame yet burns in that holy place. And Cernunnos, the horned god, walks among beasts of the field and forest, even as Saint Giles did in life."

Agnes nodded slowly. "You speak truth, My Lady. There be likeness in some things. The Church has ever taken the old feasts and given them new names. Candlemas where once was Imbolc, Easter near the spring rites of old. Yet such words will fall heavy on Mother's ears… and heavier still on those of Friar Thomas."

"Aye," said Beatrix. "He is bound by his oath to the Inquisition. To him, all that is not of Rome is heresy."

"Just so," replied Agnes. "He may not see that *The Circle* turns from blood and darkness. He may see only the root, not the fruit. Yet I believe you sincere, and I believe your cause just."

"Then I shall not falter," Beatrix said, standing tall.

Mother Alice entered Agnes's workroom, her visage grave. "I have heard this discourse, My Lady, Sister. Know you not that you tread a narrow and perilous path?"

Agnes rose at once. "Mother, My Lady's heart is true, and her purpose righteous. She seeks only to bring low the heretics of *The Kindred*, even as do we. You have trusted me in weighty matters, where now, I beseech you to grant that trust once more. Lady Beatrix and I shall see this task through, with prayer to the Holy Mother and caution in all things. I shall keep you well informed—discreetly."

Mother Alice studied her a long moment, then gave a slow nod. "Very well, Sister. But we stand in treacherous lands. We believe there yet walks among us one of *The Kindred*, a hidden serpent within these walls, who may carry word to their brethren. Therefore, guard well your tongues, and weigh your company most carefully."

"Yes, Mother," Agnes replied.

And with that, the abbess turned and departed.

Sister Agnes and Lady Beatrix – A Plan

Sister Agnes was deep in thought. "We must come to a true understanding of what divides *The Kindred* from *The Circle*. We know somewhat of their rites, their gods and goddesses, and their claim of descent from the Druids of old. Yet we know not who among *The Kindred* has forsaken their dark path to follow Edwin."

"Edwin turned from the Archdruid, Sister, for he found him cruel and given to the worship of violent gods. Even as he rose against him, he knew not his true name."

"We must uncover that name, My Lady. Once we have it, we may strike at the head, and the rest shall fall away. Know you any among *The Circle*?"

"I know none, Sister. Yet there is one who might, though I doubt he is likely to help us. He is a hard and bitter man, full of pain. The Archdruid wronged him sorely, and he thirsts for vengeance, yet fear binds him fast. I speak of Martin—the stable hand."

"Then, mayhap, we ought to bring him before Alexis. She has the gift of discernment and may glean what we cannot."

"That is a perilous course, Sister. If *The Kindred* learn who Alexis truly is, they surely will kill her. Yet she is unknown to them still, and with some small change to her dress and bearing, she might pass unseen."

"Then we shall lay it before her. The choice must be hers. If she consents, and if Martin speaks, then shall we learn who among *The Kindred* turned to *The Circle*. Once known, we may entreat them to aid us."

Alexis – Martin

Alexis entered Sister Agnes's workroom and bowed her head slightly. "What would you have of me, Sister? My Lady?"

Agnes folded her hands. "We have a task for you, child—one that is dangerous and sorely burdened. You are not bound to accept it, for it is fraught with risk and may stir wrath."

Alexis's eyes narrowed. "Does it concern *The Kindred*, Sister?"

"Yes," replied Agnes. "We needs must learn who among them turned from their dark rites and followed Sir Edwin unto *The Circle*. But to learn this, you must seek words with one who is brutish and cruel."

"And who might that be, Sister?"

"Martin," said Agnes gravely. "The stable hand."

Alexis's eyes narrowed. "Aye… he is a coarse beast of a man. Fancies himself lord of all, especially over young lasses. He takes what he would, without care or leave. But he shall not take me. I warn you—should he try, he'll learn I am no meek lass to be mastered."

Lady Beatrix's voice, low and troubled, spoke then. "He did harm Cecily once. Are you certain you wish to risk it? He is strong, and not without cunning."

"My Lady," said Alexis, standing tall, "I grew up among rough brothers, and I know well how to deal with men who press where they should not. Should he try me, it shall be the last such act he attempts. I swear it."

Agnes and Beatrix exchanged a look of grave approval tinged with unease.

"Only do this if you bear no fear in your heart," Agnes said softly.

"I fear him not," Alexis replied firmly. "Tell me what is next."

Alexis shed her workday garb and donned a rough-spun cloak and worn gown, her hair tucked beneath a frayed kerchief. She altered her gait, feigning a slight limp, and headed toward the stables. There, leaning upon his pitchfork, stood Martin. His eyes, dull yet watchful, lit up as she approached.

"What seek ye, fair maid?" he called, his tone mocking, though his eyes betrayed an eager gleam.

"I ken you to be of *The Kindred*," she said plainly, her voice roughened for effect. It was not a question.

Martin straightened. "And if I am? What then?"

"I would join you. Holy Church gives me naught but scorn, and I've no wish to waste my days in prayer and penance. I bring news from within the cloister, if you'll take me to your master."

"The Archdruid sees not just any stray, lass," he said, stepping closer. "If I am to bring you to him, you must first… make yourself agreeable."

"And how would you have that done?" she asked, her brow arched.

"I've no doubt we could come to terms," he grinned, reaching for her sleeve.

Before his fingers found their mark, Alexis moved. Her hands, clenched tightly together, came down hard upon his outstretched wrist. The sound of snapping bone cut through the silence, followed by his howl of pain.

"God's wounds! You've ruined me, strumpet—I cannot work!"

"That's no concern of mine, *boy*," she hissed sarcastically, stepping closer. "Now take me to the Archdruid… or I'll see the other hand fares no better."

She held his gaze with the cool calm of one who had faced worse and survived.

Martin held her gaze, puzzled and aching, his thoughts troubled. Who was this bold maid who sought an audience with his master? Why did she truly wish to join *The Kindred*? Was she sent to spy on them—one of the abbey's own, feigning rebellion to gather knowledge? Or was she indeed as she seemed, discontented with Holy Church and seeking another path?

One thing Martin knew: if she were true in her intent and he failed to bring her before the Archdruid, he would suffer for his disobedience. Yet, if she were a spy and he delivered her, his suffering would be all the greater.

He made his choice swiftly—better to pass her into his master's hands and let the Archdruid judge her worth.

"Come with me then, strumpet," he growled. "We shall see my master. And mayhap you'll try to break *his* arm. If you do, he'll surely slay you."

Alexis – The Archdruid

Alexis and Martin walked the long path from the abbey's walls, past the quiet outskirts of Oxford town, until they reached the deep woods beyond. There, in a clearing ringed by ancient trees, stood the Archdruid—cloaked in heavy robes and masked in fearsome fashion. His voice rang out like thunder across the glade:

"Who bring you hither, Martin?"

"This young maid seeks to join us. She bears hatred for the Church."

The Archdruid turned his masked gaze upon Alexis. "And how come you to know of us, girl? Who sent you to Martin?"

She held his gaze, steady and sharp. "All know of you. He speaks too freely. I do not. The sisters within the abbey trust me well enough."

"And will you tell us what you know?" The Archdruid's tone softened to a velvet softness that cloaked the threat beneath.

"Indeed, I will," she replied. "But I would have my due, should I aid you."

"And what is your due, child?"

"I shall give information—if I am given the same in return."

The Archdruid cocked his head. "What have you to offer, then?"

"That, my lord Archdruid," she said coldly, "is for your ears alone." Her eyes cut to Martin, who stood behind her, cheeks stained with tears, his injured wrist purple and swollen.

"Be gone, Martin!" the Archdruid bellowed.

"Aye, Master." The stable hand slunk away, limping and cradling his wrist, his pride wounded more than his body, as he made his way back toward the abbey.

With a withering gaze, the Archdruid fixed his eyes upon Alexis. "And what be your name, girl?"

"That matters not. Give me what I seek, and you shall have your due."

"Nay. You shall tell me who you are, and prove your worth, else I give you nothing."

"I shall not speak my name until I have what I came for, as I said."

"Very well," he growled. "Speak your desire."

"I seek the names of those who forsook *The Kindred* and fled to *The Circle*. They are traitors, and I would see them punished."

"And what give you in return?"

"Something you must know—your very existence, and that of *The Kindred*, hangs upon it."

The Archdruid narrowed his eyes. From within his dark cloak, he withdrew a small parchment, folded and sealed with a strange black wax. "Here is your due, girl. Now, what give you in return?"

"The inquisitor—Friar Thomas—knows who you are. And he is coming for you."

"By the Old Gods!" the Archdruid roared, striking the tree beside him with his staff. "That cannot be! How comes he by this knowledge?"

"I told you, Master Archdruid. Martin speaks more than he ought."

"Then he shall speak no more. I shall see to it myself! Now go. You have what you came for. But mark me, you shall not join us. You are not to be trusted."

Alexis offered no reply. With the parchment clutched tightly in her hand, she turned and vanished into the woods, her task complete.

Not long after, she returned to the abbey, the parchment still warm in her grasp. Straightway, she made for Sister Agnes's workroom.

The Undersheriff – Arrests

Lady Beatrix entered the undersheriff's quarters, a most humble and ill-kept place in the heart of Oxford town. At once, it was clear that the undersheriff dwelt not in luxury. The main chamber was a tangle of clutter—parchments heaped in untidy stacks, a rough-hewn worktable, and two stiff-backed chairs. Against one wall lay a narrow bed, its straw mattress worn and patched, and a hearth that served both for cookery and warmth, though it looked unused for many a season. A crude board served as a place to prepare his meals.

The dwelling was framed of timber, and the spaces betwixt filled with coarse spackling, though poorly, for the chill of the spring air crept in unbidden. Toward the back, the only structure of stone revealed itself—a gaol, stark and cold, now empty. Yet there was no sign of the undersheriff.

Beatrix turned to go, but her groom stepped forward from where he had waited beside the carriage. "My Lady," he said, "the undersheriff's constable bade me give you this missive. Will you read it?"

"Of course," she replied, taking the folded parchment. She read aloud softly, her eyes scanning the parchment. "He writes that he is abroad near Ravenswold Hall, where he has seized some of *The Kindred*. He asks that I remain here and await his return." She stepped back outside toward the carriage. "This promises to be of interest," she murmured.

Not long after, the undersheriff arrived, weary and wind-worn, accompanied by several men-at-arms. With them were three ragged prisoners, grim of face and foul in smell, whom they led to the stone cells at the rear of the house.

"We caught these knaves prowling near Ravenswold Hall, My Lady," said the undersheriff. "Perchance you will know them. Look you close, if it please you."

Beatrix stepped forward, studying each man's face in turn. "I have what is needed to bring them before both the Church and the King's justice," the undersheriff said firmly. "They have confessed themselves as members of *The Kindred* and did admit to being present at the failed sacrifice on Samhain. And hang they shall," he said, his voice like stone.

Beatrix gave him a curious look. "Then why summon me hither, sir, if their guilt be already spoken and writ?"

"It is ever useful to gather further evidence, My Lady," said the undersheriff. "And I thought, perchance, you might lend your aid."

"Well, I know them not, Master Undersheriff. I must return to the manor house ere darkness sets in. These woods are no place to linger once the sun has dipped beneath the trees."

As her carriage rumbled along, expertly guided by her young groom, Lady Beatrix mused aloud. "The one with the injured hand... he seems familiar to me. I am certain I have seen him before."

The following day, a man-at-arms from the undersheriff's retinue came to Aylesbridge Manor.

"The undersheriff bids you come to his chambers, My Lady. The prisoner—the one with the wounded hand—requests to see you. He says he has information of great worth but will share it only with you."

"Very well. Return you to the undersheriff and tell him I shall come anon." She summoned her steward. "Have the groom bring round my carriage. He shall drive me to Oxford town at once."

When she arrived at the undersheriff's humble quarters, she found him already with the prisoner. Upon seeing the man, she was certain of her memory.

"So," she said, coolly, "you claim to have tidings for me?"

"I do, My Lady—but for your ears alone."

"Very well. Master Undersheriff, I would have a word in private. Leave us but place your men outside the door to ensure my safety. And see the prisoner remains bound."

When the undersheriff departed, Beatrix turned her gaze upon the man. "Speak then, and say truth, for your life may well hang upon your words."

"I know who the Archdruid is, My Lady."

"Well then—speak, and do not dally."

"Nay, not 'til I am freed and returned to my home. I will not speak else."

"Then you shall not speak at all. Guards—take him back to the cells. He has naught of worth to tell."

"Aye, My Lady," replied the undersheriff. "A waste of your time, I fear. He shall be tried as the others."

As Lady Beatrix departed, her thoughts turned once more to the prisoner. *What knowledge might he possess that he thinks could save him from the noose?*

Chapter 23
The Godstow Witch

In which Sister Agnes and her allies confront the truth about the Godstow witch, the sect, and a crazed murderer. A surprise awaits, and the ecclesiastical courts move swiftly to seek justice.

Lady Beatrix departed the undersheriff and made her way toward Godstow Abbey. A heaviness lay upon her heart, for she needed to speak with Sister Agnes of her encounter with Martin, the stable hand. As she drew nigh the abbey's portal, she saw that it stood open, and a novice stood sentinel there.

"A fair day to you, My Lady," the novice said with a bow. "What brings you to our cloisters this day?"

"I would speak with Sister Agnes on a matter of some weight."

"As you will, My Lady. This way, I pray—"

"There is no need," Beatrix interjected gently. "I know the way to her workroom well enough." Without further word, she passed through the garden paths to Sister Agnes's chamber, arriving as Agnes rose from her worktable.

"A good day to you, My Lady. To what do I owe the honour of your visit?"

Lady Beatrix – Sister Agnes and Alexis

"I have just come from the gaol. I met the man who once tried to accost Alexis—Martin. I recognized him by the wound to his hand. He claims to know the Archdruid's true name… but will speak it only if I arrange for his release."

"So, he would not speak plain?" Agnes sighed. "That is most unfortunate."

Just then, Alexis entered the room, her brow darkened with resolve.

"A good day to you both, My Lady, Sister. So, you have seen Martin? Whatever he told you, I would wager it be false."

"Mayhap, Alexis," Beatrix replied. "But mayhap he does speak some truth, and if he truly knows the Archdruid's name, it may be what brings *The Kindred* to ruin."

Agnes folded her arms, deep in thought. "Indeed. If that knowledge lies within him, we dare not let it go untapped. My Lady, do you think the undersheriff would grant his release?"

"Perhaps," Beatrix said slowly, "but what if he deceives us and knows naught?"

"Then," Agnes said with quiet resolve, "we shall learn the truth —and deal with him accordingly."

Sister Agnes - The Godstow Witch

Agnes was quiet. Very quiet. "My Lady, think you that there was, forsooth, one behind our cloistered walls who called herself 'witch'?"

"Nay, Sister. Cecily was a heretic, for cert, but no witch was she."

Alexis added, "Aye, My Lady. In the forests, we know those called witches to be women of age and learning. They are purveyors of medicinal herbs. They are midwives. They cure the sick beasts that they may continue to provide food, milk, and labour as we plow the fields. They are gentle souls who worship no violent gods of fire and the Pit."

"This tale we needs must tell Mother. We must convince her that this terror is nearly at an end. It only remains that we unmask the Archdruid and end his reign. The rest surely will flee, or Friar Thomas and the undersheriff will capture them."

Beatrix – The Undersheriff

Lady Beatrix ascended her carriage and bade her groom take her unto the undersheriff's house, seeking thereby to obtain the release of Martin and to wrest from him the truth of *The Kindred* and the one who led them. Upon arrival at the low-built dwelling that served both as gaol and lodging, her groom alighted and offered his hand. She stepped down with measured grace and made her way toward the entrance, her mind already bent upon the means by which she might sway the undersheriff to her cause.

She entered a dim chamber at the fore of the house and took swift note of its bareness. No food lay upon the shelves, no vessel nor dish was visible, and the bed in the corner appeared long forsaken. *How strange,* she thought. *As though the man neither dwells nor labours here.*

Even as she weighed this, the undersheriff emerged from the rear passage that led to the gaol cells. "A fair day to you, My Lady," he said, with a short nod. "What brings you to my humble threshold?"

Beatrix replied, "I come seeking the release of the prisoner, Martin, that I may examine him further concerning *The Kindred* and their doings."

"That shall prove most difficult," the undersheriff said. "He needs must stand before the judge ere long, and I'll not have him vanish on my watch."

At that moment, Friar Thomas entered behind her, his voice sharp with authority. "Mayhap you forget, Master Undersheriff, that these men stand accused of heresy most foul. They have bowed before gods born of darkness. The Church shall have the first hearing, as is right and proper. Afterward, let the Crown do as it will."

"Thank you, Master Friar," the undersheriff said, his tone thick with mock courtesy. "It shall be as you decree. Lady Beatrix, the prisoner is yours for the nonce—but mind, his keeping now rests upon your good name. When your inquiry ends, see him returned to my gaol."

"So shall it be," said Beatrix with cool resolve. "Friar Thomas, you shall take the prisoner into your custody and deliver him unto Godstow. There, I shall put to him the questions which he must answer."

"As you command, My Lady," said the friar.

A moment later, the prisoner came forth, his wrists bound in iron. Under watchful guard, Martin passed into the friar's charge, and the company took the road to the abbey.

Martin – Gone from the Abbey

The friar dismounted from his black courser, the beast broad of chest and restless beneath the reins. With his guards, he led the shackled Martin into the abbey, where Lady Beatrix and Mother Alice accompanied them. Once within Sister Agnes's workroom, the guard struck off Martin's irons and departed, leaving the prisoner to the charge of Agnes, Lady Beatrix, and the Abbess.

Beatrix began at once. "Speak, Martin, of the sundering between *The Kindred* and those who call themselves *The Circle*."

"They're torn apart, My Lady," Martin said. "The Archdruid scorns *The Circle*—calls 'em weak and hollow. They don't call on the strong gods of blood and flame, but soft ones—gods of light and healing. Mark me, the fighting won't end while both sides still stand."

"Now speak his name," said Beatrix, her voice like flint. "The Archdruid, Martin. If you value your life, speak only truth."

Martin shifted uneasily. "I know not, My Lady."

"You are here, and not in the undersheriff's gaol, for that promise. Did you lie?"

At once, Martin sprang from his stool and made for the abbey's entrance. "Open the door," he bellowed, "if ye value your life!".

The novice stationed at the portal, stricken with fear, fled from her post. Martin flung the door wide, and ere Agnes or the others could give chase, he was gone into the grey light beyond.

Martin and the Archdruid

Slinking through the thickening dusk, Martin crept toward his wretched hovel on the edge of Oxford town. Friar Thomas, forewarned by Lady Beatrix that Martin might attempt to flee, acted swiftly, gathered three of his stoutest men, and led them to the place where they now crouched in the shadows to await his return.

Softly, the friar spoke. "For cert, he must come hither — if not to hide, then to ready himself for flight. We shall bide our time and follow close, yet unseen, that we may learn his purpose."

They waited not long. Soon enough, Martin slipped through the gathering gloom and into his poor abode. Like the undersheriff's, his house was mean, weather-worn, and little kept. Ere long, he emerged once more, a cruel blade now girded at his side. Hugging the shadowed brush that lined the road, he stole away toward the woods, where *The Kindred* oft wrought their rites beneath the veil of night.

Thomas and his men followed at a measured pace, keeping well behind.

Martin entered the glade where once a great fire had cast its hellish glow across the clearing. There, at the edge of the ring of small stones, stood the Archdruid.

"So, Martin," came the voice, low and mocking, "ye've escaped your gaolers, have ye?"

"Aye, I have, Master," Martin said, stepping forward, slow and careful. His voice softened with each pace, the air between them charged with dread. The Archdruid, cloaked in black and masked in gold, took little heed of Martin's creeping advance.

When he stood within reach, Martin drew the blade in a flash and drove it hard into the Archdruid's breast. The man staggered to his knees.

"No more shall ye scorn me... no more shall I name you 'Master'!" he cried. With another brutal thrust, the blade sank deep. Blood spilled. Still not content, Martin raised the weapon high and, with one final stroke, struck the head clean from the body.

Before the stable hand could recover his footing, Friar Thomas and his men emerged swiftly from the cover of the trees.

"You may have done a justice, boy," the friar growled, "but murder remains murder—and murder stains the soul. You shall answer for it."

Then, with solemn purpose, Friar Thomas stepped forward. Grasping the fallen man's head, he held it—and lifted away the fierce golden mask.

The undersheriff!

Epilogue
The Last Whisper of the Godstow Witch

In which the trials reveal lingering mysteries, and Agnes, Isabel, Beatrix, and Mother Superior begin to question the origins of The Kindred and whether its influence endures.

With the death of the undersheriff—known also as the Archdruid and master of *The Kindred*—the sect did seem, for a time, scattered and broken. Many of its former adherents, Martin the stable hand among them, stood trial and met the gallows for murder and attempted murder.

Yet testimony in both civil and ecclesiastical courts gave rise to darker fears: that some among *The Kindred*, craftier and more elusive, had gone to ground before the noose found their necks. Whispers spread—rumours of a new sect, a rekindling of that same old fire, worshippers again bowing to the dark gods of the Pit.

Sister Agnes – Speculations

Within the abbess's chamber, Agnes, Isabel, Beatrix, and Mother Alice sat in quiet counsel.

"Mother," said Agnes, "have you heard the talk—that the trials uncovered signs of a new sect paying homage to the dark ones of the Pit?"

"It may be so, Sister," the abbess replied. "We know The Adversary walks ever near, ever seeking whom he may ensnare."

Beatrix leaned forward. "But Mother, what are we to do? How shall we put an end to this reign of pain and dread?"

"I know not, My Lady," said the abbess. "We needs must be vigilant, aye—but what more lies within our power?"

"We have some means yet." Agnes's voice was firm. "We now discern the signs. We know the shape of this heresy. Yet I fear these whispers will breed unrest within our cloisters—and mayhap in the town as well. *The Kindred* was the child of the undersheriff. He named himself Archdruid and High Sacrificer, and ruled by fear and blood. Should another step forth with like ambition, he too may gather blasphemers to his cause."

Mother Alice fell silent, her gaze heavy with thought. "Let us not forget, Sister—we never did recover the full *Codex Obscura*. Only those few foul leaves found in Cecily's chamber came back to us. That book may yet lie in wicked hands. If so, another may well arise to imitate the undersheriff and seek to perform abominations akin to his."

Isabel cast her eyes downward to the chamber's stone floor. Slowly, she looked up. "Mother," her voice low and heavy with sorrow, "why would the undersheriff betray us so? Five years past he stood as our closest ally. He walked beside us through every step of our last inquiry. We placed our trust in him. Now he has turned against us, bearing arms as our foe."

"I know not, Isabel," the abbess replied gravely.

Agnes's brow grew dark. "We broke bread with him. We held back naught. All we knew, we shared. Yet all the while, he wore two faces. He stood with us by day, though by night…"

Beatrix's hands lay clenched in her lap. "I spoke with him oft. I laid bare my fears, and he hearkened unto me with nods and soft-spoken words. I never thought to doubt him—I believed he sought justice." She shook her head. "But he played us false."

"There is no shame in trust, my daughters," said Mother Alice gently. "The fault lies not in faith, but in not discerning when faith is wrongly placed."

Beatrix, still troubled, asked, "But, why think you the undersheriff founded *The Kindred*? If we know the cause, mayhap we shall learn where next to look for such a sect."

"My Lady, I see but one reason—power. The undersheriff deemed himself the true hand of justice yet bore none of the sheriff's authority. Friar Thomas found his true dwelling—a forsaken manor beyond the town bounds—furnished richly, with ornaments and fine tapestries. Mayhap he took them from rogues, who stole them from their victims. 'Tis why his chambers in town lay barren."

"There be many such as he, Mother," said Isabel. "If we seek men who hunger for power, we shall find no shortage."

"Cert, you speak true, child," said Mother Alice. "But not all who crave power turn to the fiends of the Pit. There be few so lost as that."

Alexis stepped into the chamber. "Forgive me, Mother—I stood without the door and heard your talk. This task, I can undertake. I know the faces of men who speak false, and I can read the truth writ in their deeds. If any may find the next stirrings of heresy, it is I."

"Alexis, you speak true," said Agnes. "This task falls to all of us, yet you have a gift, that is certain. You may go freely among the townsfolk and hear what they speak in corners where habits of secrecy thrive. Let us remain ever wary—another abomination shall surely follow.

The women stood and made ready to depart for their chambers, yet Beatrix lingered.

"Sister," she said softly, her eyes focused upon the floor of the chamber, "I would have a word with you."

"Of course, My Lady," said Agnes, her tone warm. "Come back with me to my workroom. We shall take tea, and you may speak what's on your heart, in quiet."

Together, they walked through the cloister garden. The evening was gentle, and they passed in silence beneath the lengthening shadows. When they arrived, Agnes poured two cups from the pot that ever hung over the hearth. After a quiet moment, she turned to Beatrix.

"Now, My Lady," said she, "what may I do to help you?"

Beatrix looked into her cup, then slowly raised her eyes to meet Agnes's.

"Sister… I am with child."

Preview

Book 3 of the
"Murders in the Abbey" Series

Death in the Convent

S ister… I am with child." Lady Beatrix's confession drew a sharp breath from Sister Agnes.

"Cert?" Agnes stumbled over her words. "You are certain? Is the father Sir Edwin?"

"Aye, Sister. That he is. At Lady Harriet's urging, I rode to Ravenswold Hall to confront him about his ties to *The Kindred*. His words were gentle, impassioned—and I believed him. He had turned away from their blasphemies, from their blood rites and madness. He had formed a new order: *The Circle of the Old Grove*, devoted to the gods and goddesses of ancient lore, not the demons of the Pit. In the glow of the great hearth in his library, we pledged our troth—and sealed it. Later that night, the Archdruid murdered him as he saved my life."

"Have you told anyone else of this?"

"No, Sister. I have not."

"Then we must move quickly and quietly. Have you evidence of your troth?"

"Aye, Sister. I have a letter in Edwin's own hand, witnessed by two reliable persons."

Meanwhile, Mother Alice dies and it becomes necessary to elect a new abbess. John Dalderby, Bishop of Lincoln, is a hard taskmaster, and he installs Maud (Matilda) Upton as the 13th abbess of Godstow Abbey. He insists that she enforce rules of discipline, enclosure (nuns not leaving the cloisters and outsiders not entering), and moral conduct. He is particularly concerned about scandal within the convent. His concern manifests in suspicion that Mother Alice was a victim of murder, a contention held by many of those in Oxford town.

Now, as the new abbess takes the reins at Godstow, the Bishop of Lincoln sends an envoy to examine the death of Mother Alice. Yet rumours stir. Whispers within the cloister and from beyond its walls cast doubt upon the election of the new abbess, and the looming birth of Lady Beatrix's child rekindles questions of inheritance, legitimacy, and the scandalous legacy of Sir Edwin de Ravenswold.

Thus begins a tale of love and loyalty, secrecy and suspicion. As Mother Maud assumes command of the abbey, she charges Sister Agnes, Isabel, Beatrix, and Alexis with uncovering the truth. What they find is a grisly secret buried deep within the cloister, seeming at first to be the work of a rogue company of Knights Templar. But Agnes soon discovers a darker revelation: one of the sisters has long harboured a hidden past, as a member of *The Kindred*. As the threads of conspiracy tighten, old fears awaken, and the peace of Godstow and Oxford town lie in the balance.

And so, Lady Harriet takes us back to her research carrel at Bodleian Library in Oxford and begins our story.

Glossary

Arbalest: A variation of the earlier crossbow. The arbalest came into use in Europe around the 12ᵗʰ century. It was a large weapon with a steel bow assembly. Since the arbalest was much larger than earlier crossbows, with the greater tensile strength of steel, it had greater force. The undersheriff's men were expert marksmen with the arbalest.

Cappa: A cape, especially as part of ecclesiastical or academic garb.

Destrier: A powerful warhorse trained for battle, used by knights, soldiers, and agents of the Holy See. Destriers were bred for strength and discipline and fit to carry warriors of God into battle or judgment.

Fey: To have supernatural powers of clairvoyance.

Garth: An enclosed quadrangle or yard, especially one surrounded by a cloister.

Grimoire: A book of arcane knowledge, rituals, spells, and sacred rites. Often bound in secrecy, grimoires serve as guides for initiates and keepers of the Old Ways. *The Codex Obscura*, grimoire of *The Kindred*, contains the most guarded instructions for their sacred ceremonies.

Humour: Body fluids. There are four recognized humours in medieval medicine: blood (sanguine), yellow bile (choleric), black bile (melancholic), and phlegm (phlegmatic).

Mote: An old subjunctive form of *may*; often used in ritual language. *So mote it be* — A ceremonial phrase meaning *"So may it be"* or *"Let it be so,"* used to affirm the completion or acceptance of a sacred act or declaration.

Nonce: The present moment or time. The time being.

Ostler: A servant who cares for horses and mules. A noblewoman such as Lady Beatrix would have at least one stable hand, also known as an ostler.

Palfrey: A docile horse used for ordinary riding, especially by women in the Middle Ages. One of Lady Beatrix's riding horses was a white palfrey.

Quarrel: A short, heavy, square-headed arrow or bolt used in a crossbow or arbalest.

Rouncey: A general-purpose riding horse commonly used by squires, men-at-arms, or poorer knights. Though not generally used by the nobility, Lady Beatrix specifically chose a rouncey for her personal riding horse.

Scry: To perceive or divine hidden knowledge or future events through ritual observation, often using reflective or translucent surfaces such as water, crystal, or obsidian. *Example: "...that we may scry the path ahead."* To see things hidden or yet to come. Practitioners gaze into a sacred surface—such as water, flame, or obsidian—to divine omens, truths, or the will of the Old Ones. The sacred black obsidian bowl, mentioned in rites, is a traditional vessel used for scrying by druids and seers.

Sigil: A symbol drawn, carved, or inscribed to channel spiritual power or summon the favor of the Old Ones. Each sigil holds specific intent—protection, summoning, binding—and must be formed with precision and will. Often hidden in plain sight or woven into ritual implements.

Stillroom: Dedicated spaces within manor houses where they distilled herbs, flowers, and botanicals and processed them for medicinal, culinary, and cosmetic purposes. They evolved from early apothecaries and alchemy laboratories.

Theriac: A medical preparation used as an antidote for any and all poisons and venom.

Turnshoe: A type of shoe constructed by sewing the upper and sole together while inside out, then turning it right side out to hide the seams.

Widdershins: To go counterclockwise.

Wroth: Intensely angry, highly incensed, or wrathful.

Historical Notes

This book is a combination of actual people and fictional characters we invented. To the best of our knowledge, none of the real individuals portrayed in this book actually performed the events or actions attributed to them. They are pure fiction, but they are based on historical descriptions of their general behavior, where we can find reliable references. Where we cite no specific sources, we have drawn from a variety of research materials, both online and in our library.

[Mother] Alice was a real person – Alice de Gorges, who, elected in 1295, served until her death in 1304. Almost nothing is known of her with the exception of her transactions as abbess as reported in *The Latin Cartulary of Godstow Abbey*, with excellent editing by Emilie Amt. This is the primary reference for transactions by the abbesses of the abbey.

Alexis is an Irish Celtic bard and seer. She wanders Oxfordshire with her family, including her maternal grandmother, Mamo, who also is a seer. She prophesies through her songs and stories. In an earlier tale, Alexis, shot by a trespasser on the king's land, was thought to be dead. She survives and goes to the abbey to become, eventually, a nun. A real person, a young singer/songwriter, inspired the character of Alexis.

[The] English Church in the 13th-14th centuries was nearly 100% Catholic. This continued until the Dissolution by Henry VIII, which took place between 1526 and 1541. The ecclesiastical hierarchy in the 13th-14th centuries appeared simple, but due to church politics, it was not simple at all. For example, inquisitors reported directly to the pope and were not part of the regular hierarchy of the Church. Additionally, a bishop from a different ecclesiastical region might overrule the local bishop if he was politically influential and had influential friends within the regular hierarchy. In fact, as you will see in our story, such bishops could bring a grievance about a person or event—even one outside their direct jurisdiction, such as an inquisitor's actions—directly to the pope or his archbishop.

The Church was highly political and sometimes made ecclesiastical appointments from outside the Church. One of the best-known examples was Thomas Becket. He was a royal chancellor before becoming Archbishop of Canterbury, although he never was a bishop or monk.

Forensic Science in England from the 12th through the 16th centuries was, at the very least, rather primitive. Although forensic science as we understand it today did not exist in the 13th and 14th-century England of our story, some learned individuals practiced principles of medical observation and postmortem reasoning, particularly within monastic infirmaries. Sister Agnes, the experienced infirmarist at Godstow Abbey, draws upon preserved classical texts to aid her understanding of illness, injury, and death. Among the most influential are the works of Avicenna and Galen (see citations below).

Book I of Avicenna's *Canon of Medicine* presents the foundational principles of medieval medical theory, including the concepts of humoral balance, organ function, and the nature of disease. This enables Sister Agnes to interpret signs of internal imbalance or failure without resorting to invasive dissection. *Book IV* addresses general diseases, wounds, fevers, and poisoning. Its practical use is important, especially when external symptoms suggest foul play.

Alongside Avicenna, Agnes references Galen, whose writings, much earlier than Avicenna's (2nd century CE), on the functions of the body and the causes of pathological change remained central to European medicine throughout the Middle Ages. Galen's insistence on close sensory observation of smell, color, and consistency of bodily excretions provides Sister Agnes with additional tools to evaluate a suspicious death. We have stayed close to these medieval and earlier resources to add realism and credibility to our story and its characters.

<u>Sources: (From books in our personal reference library):</u>

Avicenna. *The Canon of Medicine: Book I, General Principles.* Translated by Laleh Bakhtiar, Kazi Publications, 2006.
Avicenna. *The Canon of Medicine: Book IV, On General Diseases.* Translated by Laleh Bakhtiar, Kazi Publications, 2007.
Galen. *On the Natural Faculties.* Translated by Arthur John Brock, Harvard University Press, 1916.

[Lady] Harriet FitzAlan, comprising both the 21st century and 14th century characters, is and is not a real person. However, the co-author of this book inspired and created both Harriets. The book's co-author, Lady Harriet, is a real Lady of the Manor under English law. She is neck-deep in genealogy, has written a family history that goes back to her roots on the Isle of Man, and has provided editing, "medievalizing" our writing, her own contributions, and blending our voices so that the story speaks as one author, a very tricky thing to pull off. Her 21st-century Harriet is very much like the real Lady Harriet, while her fictional 14th-century Harriet is a well-imagined ancestor. Look for Lady Harriet in future books in the "Murders in the Abbey" series.

Henry de Thisteldon was, in fact, the actual sheriff of the counties of Berkshire and Oxfordshire. He was, likely, a man given to political ascension and hobnobbing with the nobility. His fictional undersheriff, Alric the Bald, did all the actual enforcement of the law.

For more on Alric, see the blog at
<u>https://murdercanbefun</u>.net/blog/f/an-interview-with-undersheriff-alric-the-bald.

[The] Kindred was not a real sect, though it reflects characteristics of certain clandestine spiritual and heretical movements of the period and those that followed. We have taken some literary license with this one. While *The Kindred* claims a Druidic heritage, there is little to no evidence that Druidic behavior, as reported by Romans—such

as Julius Caesar and Tacitus—came anywhere near *The Kindred's* demon worship and human sacrifice. The Druids were not a tribe or people, but the priestly and intellectual class among the ancient Celts. Their beliefs were closely tied to nature, and their deities represented the forces of land, sea, and sky. The Romans eventually suppressed Druidic practices; the full eradication of their influence likely took generations. Today, there are modern Druidic groups that echo the ancient times.

Sources:

Green, Miranda J. *The World of the Druids*. Thames & Hudson, 1997.

Ellis, Peter Berresford. *The Druids*. William B. Eerdmans Publishing Company, 1994.

Lucid Dreaming: We shaped some elements of this story through a phenomenon we call a *temporal shift*. It is a rare experience reported by lucid dreamers. In the dream, the dreamer becomes fully aware within it and may observe or even step into the life of another person, sometimes one from the distant past. In Lady Harriet's case, these dreams allow her to witness and ultimately inhabit the life of her 14th-century ancestor, also named Harriet.

While we make no claim to actual time travel, the experience draws on documented phenomena in lucid dreaming research and on historical notions of ancestral memory. The shifts serve not only as a narrative bridge between centuries but also as a way of exploring identity, memory, and the powerful connection we feel to those who came before us.

Sources:

LaBerge, S. (1985). Lucid Dreaming. Ballantine Books.

Hurd, R., & Bulkeley, K. (Eds.). (2014). Lucid Dreaming: New Perspectives on Consciousness in Sleep. ABC-CLIO.

Mary Wood, the librarian in the Bodleian Library of the University of Oxford, is a fictional character. However, she is based upon a very real person, Mrs. Mary I Wood, who was the librarian at a private girls' school in Indianapolis, Indiana. In addition, she taught English History and instilled a love of both reading and research in her students.

Rewley Abbey and Godstow Abbey were real cloisters. Both Rewley Abbey and Godstow Abbey have fallen into ruin over the centuries. Those ruins, however, are available to visit today. The rituals depicted at the abbey—and, more broadly, those of the Catholic Church, which held power in England until the reign of Henry VIII—we abbreviated for readability. They are simplified versions of the actual rites practiced at the time. We have used Latin, the language of the Church, sparingly for realism, and when we have used it, the scene includes English translations.

Witches and heresy may be similar in the modern world, but in medieval times, they were not. Witches – a rare term – were old "wise women". Of course, "old" had an entirely different meaning in the 13th and 14th centuries. These women usually chose to live relatively solitary lives, acting as midwives, healers, herbalists, and the like. The term "witchcraft" came into ecclesiastical use beginning in the 14th century and matured after the 15th-century publication of The Malleus Maleficarum ("Hammer of the Witches") by Dominican inquisitors Heinrich Kramer and Jakob Sprenger, although scholars debate Sprenger's role.

Acknowledgements

It can be challenging to remember all of the fine folks who contributed to the creation of this story. If we leave anyone out, please know that we appreciate your support and look forward to working with you on future projects.

Our appreciation and gratitude go out to Dee Marley, our long-suffering publisher, advisor, and marketing guru. After spending what must have been an inordinate amount of time editing Book 1 of our series, we thought that perhaps she had had enough and would suggest that we find another publisher. But, no. With infinite patience, she tackled *"The Witch…"* and even signed us to a third book plus the companion volume for Books 1 and 2. This volume will help place you in a 14th-century frame of mind.

Special thanks go to Craig Stephen Copland, mystery writer extraordinaire. Craig has written around 100 books—about 60 of them are Sherlock Holmes pastiches—most of which Dr. Stephenson had the pleasure of beta-reading. Craig generously returned the favor by offering us a thoughtful critique of this book, and we have incorporated many of his suggestions. The book, we are certain, is much the better for his input.

We also wish to thank Ms. Sunny Bleau, a Memphis blues recording star, and her husband, Nic Cocco, who have provided valuable ideas and encouragement throughout the process of writing Book 2. Dr. Stephenson spent many hours discussing the similarities between the publishing world and the music business. We were able to consider many of his observations to our – and the book's – benefit.

Another shoutout goes to Dr. Stephenson's lodge brothers in Masonic lodge, F&AM, Utica-Macomb #64, for a long conversation in which many suggestions came up as well as questions that caused

Dr. Stephenson to consider some of the plot issues with this story. Again, the book is better for their input.

We selected a diverse group of beta readers, including male and female authors, educators, and friends who simply love to read. We cannot thank you enough for taking the time to be part of our process and providing your thoughts, insights, and eagle eyes for grammar. Thank you to Craig Copeland, Kelly Brock, Ann Tinkham, Judy Dukes, Lee Guertin, Toni Massar, Jerry McWilliams, Tammy Schultz, Rob Givens, Erin Swann, and Charlene Hamood.

And, finally, we would like to thank our families and friends. There aren't words enough to express the appreciation we have for your unwavering support and love, particularly your understanding and patience with our many absences, delayed replies, and distracted minds. Thank you for forgiving the missed birthdays, the unanswered texts, the rain checks on dinners, and the social events we fully intended to attend, but didn't. For the golf games unplayed, the exercise classes skipped, and the phone calls we cut short with a "Can I call you right back?"—we apologize. Your grace made space for this book. We are forever grateful.

About the Authors

Lady Harriet Taggart

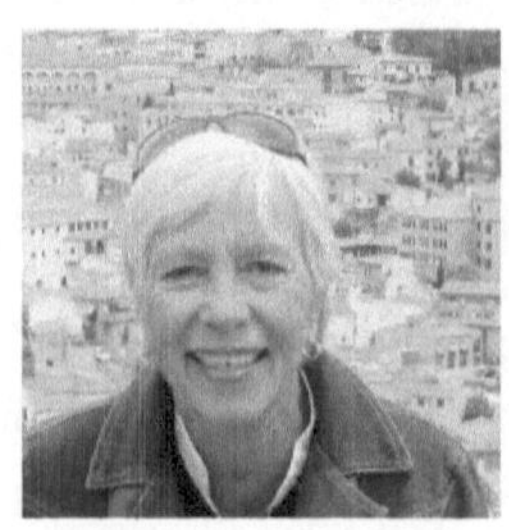

Lady Harriet holds the legal title "Lady of the Manor," as defined under English law, and traces her ancestry to Charlemagne's royal line.

A lifelong reader and devoted genealogist for nearly fifty years, Harriet has always had a passion for stories, whether they are buried in the past or found in the pages of a good book. She is the co-author of *We Are Manx*, a self-published family saga that explores her Manx heritage and the history of the Isle of Man in rich detail.

She's also a photographer who prefers being behind the lens, a word lover addicted to word games, and a fan of wooden jigsaw puzzles. She has traveled extensively, with a deep appreciation for history, diverse cultures, and the unexpected joys that can be found away from home. Her career spanned volunteerism, real estate, and systems administration, but now she happily devotes her time to more creative pursuits.

As she puts it: "I'm old enough for Medicare, but not quite old enough to get a birthday card from King Charles—were I a Brit."

The Witch of Godstow Abbey, written in partnership with Dr. Peter Stephenson, marks her first (but hopefully not last) foray into historical fiction. With photography, she creates books of images; with storytelling, she creates images made of words.

Dr. Peter Stephenson

Dr. Stephenson has written or contributed to over twenty books, all but one of which are non-fiction technical books. He has published over 1,000 papers in technical journals, technical trade journals, and peer-reviewed legal journals. One of his peer-reviewed papers has over 15,400 downloads.

In addition to writing, Dr. Stephenson has been playing blues and Americana music for 70 years. It is through that performing, and after earning a PhD from Oxford Brookes University, that he was given the appellation "Doc" by the owner of one of his performance venues.

Having visited Oxford several times and being employed by a UK company in nearby Malvern, it was only natural that he would set his tales in Oxfordshire. His academic experience in Oxford town sealed the deal and resulted in his first historical novel, *The Whispering Dead of Rewley Abbey*— Book 1 in the "Murders in the Abbey" series— which reached the Amazon Kindle best seller list and won a Pencraft award for literary excellence in the winter of 2025. He now writes with his collaborator and writing partner, Lady Harriet.

Dr. Stephenson lives with two Savannah cats on a pond in Auburn Hills, Michigan. Starting a "new" career at the age of 80, Doc reckons that he has only about the next 20 years to finish the series and retire – again – perhaps this time to Oxford.

www.historiumpress.com

www.ingramcontent.com/pod-product-compliance
Lightning Source LLC
Chambersburg PA
CBHW061246310726
48971CB00007B/2246